HAPPY TAILS DOG WALKING MYSTERIES

Barking up the
Wrong Bakery

Till Death do us
Bark

One Bark and Stormy
Prom Night

and to be continued...

Barking up the Wrong Bakery

Stella St. Claire

BLURB

Some people would kill for coffee…

Olivia Rickard would kill to keep everything just the way it is. She's got a gorgeous boyfriend who loves her, a supportive sister to lean on, and a dog walking business that's briskly barking away. But just as she's getting comfortable her sister suddenly wants to buy an entire brownstone with her and her boyfriend looks like he's going to pop the question at every opportunity. Changing the status quo has always been disastrous for Olivia and now everything is changing at once…

What Olivia needs is a distraction and she's found one in stumbling upon Yvette Dunn dead in her coffee foodtruck—drowned in a vat of fresh coffee. Olivia starts out as an unlucky bystander to the crime, but she's forced to dig in deeper when it looks like her sister could be involved in Yvette's death.

Olivia is running out of time in regards to the mystery, the mortgage, and the marriage. She's going to have to solve all three problems—and quick—or face a future most foul.

Thank you for purchasing 'Barking up the Wrong Bakery'

(Happy Tails Dog Walking Mysteries Series Book One)

Sign-up to Stella's mailing list at:

www.StellaStClaire.com

Connect with Stella on:

Stella's Website: www.StellaStClaire.com

Facebook: www.facebook.com/stellastclaire/

Goodreads: www.goodreads.com/Stella_StClaire

TABLE OF CONTENTS

CHAPTER ONE

The sun was barely peeking over the horizon when I walked up to the truck. *Jump Start Coffee*. It was a cute name. Cute painting on the food truck. Everything was just so perfect for the woman inside.

Lexingburg is straight out of Mayberry. I grew up here, and sometimes even I can't believe how idyllic the streets are. Everyone knows everyone. It's the type of town where we make time out of our morning schedule to speak to people as we walk or drive to work. There was a time when I wanted nothing more than to run away from it all, but eventually the town grows on you. We all lend a helping hand to those in need. It's like living in a television show. We even have town square fairs with cotton candy machines and kissing booths.

She starred in a few of those kissing booths. It curled my stomach to think of her sitting there with her bleached-blonde hair and cherry-red lips.

Those lips that did nothing but spew lies. That woman did nothing but think about her bottom line. She didn't care who she hurt.

Enough was enough. I couldn't let her poison anything else. This was my town, and it was time that she played by *my* rules. She was finally going to listen to me.

1

I walked behind the truck, ripped open the back door, and climbed in. Yvette glared at me as she pulled the basket of steaming grounds from the large vat. "What are you doing here? I'm not open yet!"

"I'm not here for coffee."

A taunting smile curved over her poisonous lips. "Don't tell me that you came here to talk."

I could feel my jaws clench as I narrowed my eyes. "I just came here to ask you to stop. Enough is enough."

"Enough is enough," she mocked. "I haven't done anything wrong, and I have no reason to back off."

I wanted to talk to her. I wanted her to see what she was doing to me, what she was doing to this town.

Yvette didn't grow up here. She didn't care about the people. She had no friends.

She was alone.

"I'm warning you," I whispered.

Straightening, she glared at me. "I'm not going to stop, so you might as well just give it up."

"Give it up?" I hissed. "Do you have any idea what you're doing?"

She smiled coldly at me. "I know exactly what I'm doing, and you'd better stay away from me!"

I don't know what happened. One minute I was standing by the door, and the next, I had her hair in my hands and plunged her face into the boiling liquid. It was like something out of a dream. I didn't hear her screams, though in hindsight, she must have. I don't remember a struggle. It was so simple, so elegant, just holding her in place, letting her get a really good idea of how foul her coffee was.

When she slumped over, I eased her to the floor. A mess. I'd made a mess. Grabbing the mop in the corner, I cleaned up. Coffee beans were spilled all over the counter. When did that happen? I didn't even remember being on that side of the truck. I didn't even remember drowning her.

No fingerprints. No mess.

When I finished, I grabbed a couple of scones from the tray and carefully stepped over the body. It was only then that I saw the sun glinting on the object that had fallen in the struggle. Bending down to pick it up, I inspected it with a slow smile.

No one was anyone near the food truck when I walked away.

It wasn't until later that I felt the pain. The coffee had splattered and burned me. Funny how overpowering the adrenaline from taking a life could be. I felt unstoppable. Nothing would keep me from protecting what was mine.

CHAPTER TWO

Rose Palmer crept around the corner, holding the frying pan in her hand. The room was pitch black, and nervous sweat dripped down her back as her nightgown clung to her body. She could still hear the fumbling sounds of the thief as he pawed through her drawers. Was he looking for the documents? How did he know that she had them?

More importantly, what would he do when he discovered that she didn't need them anymore?

The dogs barked sharply, and Olivia Rickard jumped. She was immediately pulled out of her dark world of mystery and back into the sunny park.

"Are you listening to me?" Andrew asked casually.

Cringing inwardly, Olivia tried to discreetly pull her ear bud out of her ear. Her boyfriend had the day off and wanted to spend it with her, even if that meant joining her on her dog walks, and while she loved him and enjoyed spending time with him, this was her alone time. Her time to listen to music and snag another chapter from her audiobook.

After years of searching for the necklace, Rose was another step closer to finding it. That necklace was her only link to her grandmother!

Rose Palmer was the main character in Olivia's favorite mystery series, *The Palmer Files.* The young and spunky private investigator was everything Olivia believed in. Rose traveled whenever the mood struck, she didn't have to follow anyone's rules, and she was *brilliant.* In the last book, Rose took down a murderer and an abusive boyfriend. Now, in *The Necklace of Deceit,* Rose searched desperately for her grandmother's missing emerald necklace, but it led her closer and closer to a dangerous secret society. Olivia had started the book two weeks ago, but every time she tried to listen to it, another interruption came along.

"Olivia!"

"I'm listening," she said grumpily as she looked up. She *was* listening, but it was a conversation that she really didn't want to have.

Goodwin barked and pulled against the leash, and, as usual, the other dogs followed. She was supposed to be a professional dog walker, owner of Happy Tails Dog Walking, but it was her own mangy mutt that constantly led the pack into trouble. How embarrassing was that?

She couldn't even control her own dog. Snapping her fingers, she tried to get his attention.

Her boyfriend continued talking as if Goodwin wasn't acting like a maniac. "So is it okay if we make the reservations for

L'Amore at eight, or do you still need to stop by the Garners' and give their dog his medicine?"

L'Amore was easily the fanciest—and priciest—restaurant in town. It was on the tip of her tongue to grab the excuse he'd given her, but Andrew would only push the dinner reservations back. Besides, the Garner family had returned from vacation yesterday, and she couldn't lie to Andrew.

"Why do you want to have a fancy dinner on a Thursday night? We both have early mornings tomorrow. Are we celebrating something?"

Her words were a little harsher than she'd anticipated, and he looked wounded. His eyes widened and his mouth opened slightly, but he hesitated before speaking. "We haven't had much alone time, and I wanted to do something nice for you."

"This is because of the conversation we had a couple of months ago, isn't it?" She searched his face. Olivia didn't usually date men for longer than six months. When she'd managed to push through their six-month anniversary, Andrew had asked her to move in with him. In a moment of panic, she'd told him that she didn't feel right moving in with a man before marriage. Even though they spent several nights a week together, it was important that she had her own space.

Just in case.

"I told you that I respected your position, and I do," he said softly. "Olivia, this has nothing to do with that. I just want to take you to a nice dinner. One that doesn't involve frozen pizza and cheap beer. A romantic evening."

"I *like* frozen pizza and cheap beer," she said, then smiled and leaned up to kiss him. She was about to agree, but she was still terrified of what a fancy dinner for no reason might mean.

The proposal of a lifetime.

"Yoo-hoo! Olivia!"

The voice came from behind her, but Olivia didn't have to turn around to see who it was. The high-pitched whine could only come from Lady Celeste Rhoda, the local psychic.

A pained expression crossed Andrew's face, and it was all Olivia could do not to laugh as she turned around.

"Lady Celeste, how can I help you?" she asked pleasantly, smiling at the woman hurrying to join them. Celeste claimed Romanian roots, but as far as Olivia knew, the woman had no ties to aristocracy. Olivia always wanted to ask if Lady was her first name rather than a title.

The woman had wrinkles that belonged to a grandmother, but the thick and lustrous shiny hair of a teenager. She looked exactly the same as she had the first time Olivia had met her, over two decades ago. She dressed in bright, vivid dresses and always covered her head with a color-coordinated scarf.

When she stopped, she wobbled slightly as though she weren't used to chasing after people. Spreading her arms dramatically in welcome, she bent down to coo at the dogs. "Good morning, Goodwin. How are you feeling today? I can see that you're very excited. This leash is holding you back, isn't it? You want to run free with your companions!"

Celeste was an unusual woman, but she didn't usually talk to the dogs. Or *for* the dogs. Olivia exchanged a puzzled look with Andrew. "It's illegal to walk the dogs without a leash," she pointed out.

"I know that, but Goodwin doesn't understand! That's what I wanted to talk with you about. I'd like to dedicate a segment of my day for the pets of Lexingburg. Would you please spread the word?"

It was all Olivia could do not to laugh. "I'm sorry, Lady Celeste. I'm not sure that I understand. You want to talk to the pets?"

"I want to communicate the pets' wishes to the owners. Just imagine how much happier everyone will be when their thoughts and desires are communicated properly. I can see that there's tension between you and Goodwin. Perhaps you should stop by!"

Then, like a sign from above, Olivia's phone vibrated.

"I'll keep that in mind, and I'll be sure to spread the word. Please excuse us. This could be important," Olivia said as she pulled out her phone. The dogs pulled impatiently at their leashes before she snapped her fingers. They grumbled but stopped and waited for her. Looking down at her text messages, she groaned.

It was not the distraction she'd wanted.

"Is that Janelle?" Andrew asked, giving her a quizzical look. Celeste was already fluttering her arms down Main Street, an unlikely butterfly, as she headed to her small shop. "Have you started the paperwork yet to buy the brownstone?"

Fancy dinners. Buying office space. And to think that she'd had such high hopes for today. The weather was warm, and the sun was shining. The mystery in her book was deepening, but she had a boyfriend threatening to propose and a sister wanting to commit to office space. Why couldn't they just be happy? Life was good just the way things were!

"No, we haven't started yet. Janelle was supposed to meet with Franklin about the sale," Olivia muttered. Franklin Kennedy owned quite a bit of real estate around town, including several of the food trucks. Janelle had been renting from him for the past two years while she got her bakery, Happy Endings, up and running, and a couple of weeks ago, Franklin had let her know that he was going to sell. He'd offered Janelle first dibs on the sale before he'd go public with the offer.

Andrew leaned over and kissed her on the top of her head. "Everything is working out for you, baby. You've been talking about office space for your dog-walking business forever, and now Janelle is offering to help you. It's perfect. A bakery downstairs, and you can expand your business upstairs."

"Yup," Olivia said uneasily. "Everything is working out."

It *was* perfect. Andrew was right. For the past few months, she'd juggled with the idea of looking for office space. The word-of-mouth operation that she was running was fine, but she couldn't advertise without an office. Her sister wanted to buy, but Janelle couldn't afford the down payment on the perfect brownstone on Main Street on her own.

Olivia had received a small settlement last year from insurance and hadn't invested it yet.

Together, they could make it work.

Except, for some reason, the idea didn't seem so perfect anymore. Olivia was paying her bills. She had a solid client base. Why mess with a good thing? But when Janelle had asked, Olivia just froze.

Her sister assumed it was from excitement and took her silence to mean yes.

And then Andrew started acting weird. Whispering about their future when he thought she was asleep. Trying to be more romantic. Last week, he'd bought her a dozen roses for no reason. The week before that, he interrupted her nightly outside reading ritual to cuddle with her on the hammock and whisper the sweetest things in her ear. It would have been adorable if she hadn't been trying to listen to Rose Palmer's exciting investigation.

Olivia could put two and two together. Andrew wasn't the kind of man to plan romantic interludes, not to mention, for weeks now, the whole town kept constantly asking when they would get married. She thought that Andrew would just shrug it off, but apparently not.

It wasn't that she didn't want to marry Andrew. She just wasn't sure that she wanted to marry him *now*, and she certainly didn't want to marry him because he was feeling pressure.

They were such a good couple. Olivia had never felt this way about anyone before. She'd never felt safe and secure in a relationship, and even after a year of dating Andrew, when she looked over at his handsome face and boyish smile, he still made her heart skip a beat.

She was happy, but he wanted more, and that was so clear now. The desire to move in together. The fancy dinner reservations. The push to solidify her dog-walking business. He was planning a life with her, and on one hand, that meant everything to her. She wanted to spend her life with Andrew.

But on the other hand, everything was so perfect now. Why change it? Why complicate it? Why risk it? If they took this step, and they weren't ready for it, it could spell d-i-s-a-s-t-e-r.

"Whoa! Goodwin," she snapped as the dogs pulled her a couple more feet forward. Jax, the yellow Labrador, was so well behaved, and even Lily, the dachshund, was good as long as there was something for her to dig in or chew on. But her giant, brown, shaggy *thing* was a troublemaker.

"Andrew, about tonight," she started as she looked behind her, but the sight froze her blood. He was bending to one knee with a mischievous smile on his face.

Here?

Now?

She was at work, with three smelly, furry, four-legged creatures pulling her in the opposite direction. For God's sake, he wasn't going to propose here, was he? Whirling around before he could ask that life-altering question, she started to run. Barking in glee, the dogs jumped into action.

"Olivia, hold up!" Andrew called out. "I think I have a broken shoelace. Hang on!"

A broken shoelace? Slowing down, she closed her eyes as embarrassment and relief washed over her. Guilt followed immediately. Was she the worst girlfriend in the world?

Pointing lamely at the Jump Start food truck across the parking lot, she grinned weakly. "Sorry. I saw that Yvette hasn't moved the truck yet, and I just really need coffee. I'll go ahead and get our order." Shaking her head at her own idiocy, she jogged the rest of the way to the truck. It wasn't in her nature to run, but the situation begged for a quick escape.

She was actually surprised to see the truck in the parking spot. Normally, at this time of day, Yvette was across town, and Olivia would have to wait until after she'd dropped the dogs off at their various homes before main-lining her caffeine addiction. The sight of the large painted cappuccino on the side of the truck warmed her to her very toes.

The service window was closed, so she raised her voice to make sure she was heard. "Yvette! I'm so glad I caught you! You have no idea how much I need my coffee. But no scone," she added as an afterthought. She'd heard Janelle ranting for the past few days that Yvette was selling Janelle's baked goods past their sale date. Olivia had thought that Yvette's goods tasted a little off, but then, she normally sampled Janelle's goodies straight from the oven. Nothing was ever as good as that.

"Andrew is with me, so he'll take his—large coffee, cream and sugar." She dropped her voice. "Actually, just make his coffee black. A little bitterness might do him some good," she muttered as she glanced behind her. Andrew was jogging toward her with his phone up to his ear.

Goodwin whined and pulled at the leash. Olivia frowned and spoke to the window again. "If you can't tell, that's Goodwin, but he's being a devil dog, so no whipped cream for him today." She glared at Goodwin sternly. "See? That's what happens when you pull. No whipped cream for you."

A few seconds of silence passed. She and Yvette weren't friends, but it wasn't like the food truck owner to ignore her. The woman enjoyed her money. "Yvette?" She reached up and knocked on the covered window. The aluminum rattled, but there was no additional noise coming from the truck.

Andrew caught up with her and sighed. "Olivia, I've got to go, sweetheart. Work just called. Apparently, they're having some problems with the computers in the surgical wing of the hospital— but I know I can still make it for dinner tonight."

Ignoring him, she handed off the leashes. "Something's wrong."

"I'm going to make it up to you," he protested.

Olivia shook her head. "Not that. Something's wrong with Yvette!"

"What are you talking about? Olivia, I have to go now. Take the dogs."

He tried to hand her the leashes, but she walked past him to the back of the truck. "She should have started her rounds hours ago," Olivia pointed out. "If she took the day off, she'd put a sign up. Yvette doesn't just abandon the truck."

"Maybe she's running late. You can get coffee after you drop the dogs off. Olivia, what are you doing?"

"I'm telling you that something is wrong. I just want to check inside." Having reached the back, she jiggled the handle on the door. Goodwin barked anxiously, and the door opened.

The switches on the coffee burners were all showing red, and the warmer for the baked goods was on. Even the small cooler in the corner was humming. The whole place smelled delicious—like coffee, of course. The food truck was ready for business, but Yvette wouldn't be serving any coffee today.

Instead, she was soaking wet—as if she'd dumped a carafe of coffee over herself—and motionless on the floor. She was dressed in a pair of jeans and a low-cut halter-top. Her long blonde hair was spread out over the floor. Yvette was in her late twenties, and it stunned Olivia to see a woman her own age lying dead on the floor. For a moment, she couldn't even breathe.

"Olivia? What are you doing?" Andrew's question jarred Olivia out of her frozen state.

Swallowing hard, Olivia turned to see Andrew, dark against the

15

open door. "Call 911," she said hoarsely. "I think Yvette is dead."

"Dead? Olivia, get out of there." Before she could protest, Andrew's hand circled her, and he lifted her easily from the truck. His phone was already out, and he handed the leashes to her. With one arm wrapped protectively around her waist, he called Sheriff Nicholas Limperos.

Goodwin yanked hard against the leash and pulled away from Olivia. "No! Goodwin, get back here!" she yelled.

"Olivia, don't go in there," Andrew ordered, but the dog had bounded into the truck and was sniffing in the corner.

"I can't just let him run wild in the truck," Olivia protested. She pushed the other two leashes into his free hand that he was holding out to restrain her, and climbed in. Leaning down to snag the leash, she couldn't help but notice the coffee beans that had rolled under the counter.

Yvette was meticulous about cleaning the food truck. Almost insanely meticulous. It didn't make sense that she hadn't swept under the counter. Immediately, Olivia's mind flashed back to a *Palmer Files* mystery book. Rose's obsessive-compulsive neighbor had allegedly committed suicide, but Rose had proven it was murder because the neighbor would never have left a mess behind.

Pulling hard, the dog yanked the leash through Olivia's hands—

16

somehow she managed to keep hold of the end of the leash—bounded to the far side of Yvette's body, and lay down. "I can't reach him without stepping over Yvette, and I don't want to disturb the crime scene," Olivia called helplessly to Andrew, still outside the open door.

Rose Palmer would never make a mistake like this. She was an amazing investigator. Just last week, Olivia had followed the fictional private investigator as she took down a crime boss. A crime boss! Rose wouldn't dare let an undisciplined dog ruin a crime scene.

Andrew hung up and peered in. "Crime scene? You don't know that a crime was committed here. Yvette could have passed away for a number of reasons. We don't exactly know her private business."

Andrew wasn't wrong, but there were some things that didn't make sense. Yvette was soaked in coffee, but she wasn't holding a coffee pot in her hand to indicate that she'd spilled coffee on herself when she fell. In fact, the place was spotless, with the exception of the coffee beans spilled on the counter and floor, but the container of beans was tucked neatly away on the counter. No dust. No spider webs. Nothing to indicate that Yvette didn't take excellent care of the truck.

Olivia also knew that Yvette carried a change of clothes in the front of the truck. The woman hated the thought of wearing just one outfit all day, and she wouldn't dare be caught with a stain. Why hadn't she changed?

Andrew was still urging Olivia to get out of the truck, but her eyes roamed over the scene as quickly as possible. There was a hole torn in the plastic covering of the scone tray, and two scones were missing. Her heart raced. Janelle was careful when she wrapped her baked goods, and even if Yvette was selling out-of-date treats, she wouldn't have ripped the plastic like that.

Someone knocked over a canister of beans and then put it away without cleaning everything up. Someone ripped open the scones and stole two before leaving. Someone poured coffee on Yvette and then put the pot away.

Her eyes strayed to the small, round coffee vat in the corner. It was covered, but there were coffee stains running down the side.

Taking a deep breath, Olivia took a few more steps closer to the body and stared at Yvette's face. There were burn marks on her skin, and her hair was soaking wet.

Immediately, she knew what had happened, and her heart sank. "Oh, Yvette." Swallowing hard, she snapped her fingers. "Goodwin. You come here right now!"

As if he understood her distress, her dog lifted his head and loped back over to her. Grabbing his leash firmly, she hopped out of the truck just as Nick's sheriff car pulled up. As she glanced up, she saw the security camera mounted to the corner of the truck, and she shivered.

"Olivia. Andrew," Nick greeted. "What's going on?"

"Sheriff. It looks like Yvette passed away in the truck," Andrew said calmly.

"She was murdered," Olivia blurted out. "Someone drowned her in her own vat of coffee."

As the two men stared at her, she glanced uneasily around her. There was a killer in their small town, and they'd murdered Yvette just hours before Olivia got there. What if they were still around, watching her?

"Olivia, I think you've been reading too many mystery books," Andrew said, laughing nervously. "This is Lexingburg. Murders don't happen in Lexingburg."

"Tell Yvette that."

CHAPTER THREE

The sheriff spent about fifteen minutes asking Andrew questions before letting him go. Andrew leaned over and kissed Olivia on the cheek. "I've got to get to work. Are you sure that you're going to be okay?"

"Go to work," she said as she pushed him slightly. "I'm fine."

He searched her face with a grim expression. "Olivia, promise me that you're going to give your statement to Nick and let him do his job. Don't interfere."

"Me? Interfere? Why on earth would I do that?"

"Because I know you. You spent all of five seconds in the truck, and you told Nick that it was murder."

"It *is* murder, but Nick is the sheriff, and I will let him do his job," she promised.

Reaching out, he squeezed her hand. "I shouldn't be at work for long, so I'll call you if I can't make it. Eight o'clock."

If there was any excuse to miss out on dinner, it would be discovering Yvette dead, but Olivia couldn't do that to Andrew. He just looked so eager. "I'll try to walk my evening dogs early. I'll talk to you later. Have a good day." Although she smiled, she knew her tone was begrudging at best.

There was disappointment in his eyes, but it was overshadowed by worry. Olivia couldn't help but feel awful. Here was the most wonderful man worrying about her, and she was dodging a romantic evening because she was afraid he was going to propose.

"I'm a terrible person," she muttered as she watched him walk away.

Nick raised an eyebrow. "What was that?"

Turning to the aging sheriff, she shook her head. "Nothing. You have some questions for me?"

"Andrew said that Goodwin jumped into the truck. Do you know if he disturbed anything?" He affectionately scratched the dog's ears and knelt to receive kisses from the other dogs. Nick and his wife Mary had their own dog, a sweet Labradoodle named Tucker. Olivia occasionally walked the dog, although Mary thought Nick was walking Tucker during his lunch breaks. She was pushing her husband to exercise more. Apparently his last doctor's appointment hadn't gone well.

"Not that I know of. He jumped into the truck, stepped over Yvette, and settled on the floor. He didn't even try to get into the treats or steal the coffee. The beans were already spilled on the counter, and I didn't see him lick anything. The place was clean. Yvette's a neat freak. More than a neat freak. She wouldn't wear

21

stained clothes, and she wouldn't leave coffee beans on the counter and floor."

"Coffee beans, huh," Nick grunted as he stood and started making notes. "It looks to me like you saw quite a bit."

Clearing her throat, she fidgeted and looked everywhere but at him. "I just wanted to make sure that my dog didn't compromise your crime scene. That's all."

"Right," he said wryly. "Olivia, I know that you love your mysteries, but this is real life."

"Sheriff," she said with a wide grin, even shrugging for good measure, "I just came here to get my coffee, and I got worried when Yvette didn't answer. I'm just guilty of being a good neighbor."

"You're always trying to be a good neighbor," Nick complained. "You're also a little nosey."

Outraged, she gasped. "I am not!"

"Two months ago, you threw a surprise party for Lydia even though she explicitly stated that she didn't want a celebration," he said calmly.

"Her husband left her. She needed something to cheer her up," Olivia pointed out. "And she had a good time."

"She screamed so loud that we all thought she was going to have a heart attack Back in November, you broke into Norman's house to confront a robber, even though there was no robber."

"It wasn't breaking in! I had a key. I was dog sitting, and his dog was trying to tell me that something was wrong. In my panic, I just forgot about the alarm code," she said stubbornly. "And something *was* wrong!"

"The fish died."

"And that upset the dog. Look, I know what you're thinking, but I promised Andrew that I wouldn't get involved, so I'm just telling you what I saw. The fact that I'm an observant person is a good thing!"

Three more squad cars pulled up, and Nick sighed and closed his notebook. "We're going to process the scene now. I'll let you know if I have any more questions, and I would appreciate it if you didn't call it a crime scene or talk to anyone else about it."

"Okay, but I just wanted to let you know that Yvette would never have opened the tray of scones that way, so maybe you'll find fingerprints on the plastic. And the coffee bean canister may have overturned in the struggle, so you might find fingerprints on that as well." She spoke so rapidly that her words ran together. She didn't want to give Nick a chance to accuse her of being nosey again before she got through all of her observations. "And if someone spilled the beans, the killer may have tried to sweep it up, so check the broom handle and the mop!"

Nick gave her a pointed look. "Olivia, I know how to do my job."

Slowly backing up, Olivia gave him a sheepish smile. "No, of course you do. I'm just going to drop off the dogs and grab some breakfast at Happy Endings. Call me if you need me."

The sheriff had already turned his back, and Olivia tried to push the sight of Yvette's body out of her mind. Of course Nick could do his job. The man was pushing fifty, and he was an excellent sheriff.

Of course, he was an excellent sheriff for Lexingburg. The biggest problem here was when someone like herself accidentally set off an alarm. People didn't get murdered here, and Nick wasn't equipped for this kind of problem.

What could it hurt if she helped?

"No," she told herself sternly. "It's not your job. You're a dog walker, and you've got a lot on your plate."

Like a sister who wanted her to buy real estate and a boyfriend who wanted to put a ring on her finger.

After dropping off Jax and Lily, it was just Olivia and Goodwin when they headed to Happy Endings. The brownstone that her sister rented was in a perfect location. Right in the middle of the row of businesses on Main Street, it sat between Shelfie, a bookstore, and Delilah's Silks, a women's boutique. It faced one of the three major crosswalks, and attracted both local and tourist clientele.

Releasing Goodwin in the small fenced-in yard out back, Olivia snuck in through the back door and snagged a scone from the cooling rack before searching for her sister. The bakery always smelled like fresh-baked cookies. When Janelle first started baking, the kitchen would be a disaster, but by the time those doors were unlocked, the place was pristine. The front of the bakery was decorated in pale creams, blues, and purples. Most of the customers chose seats on the large patio out front, but during bad weather, the small dining space inside was crowded. Janelle was an excellent baker, and her business did well.

The only problem was the building itself. It dated back to the fifties, and it had been several decades since the place had seen some repairs. While the shops on either side were updated, Janelle dealt with issues on a monthly basis, and the landlord always made the cheapest repairs possible. The roof needed fixing, but Franklin only managed patches when it started leaking. The screens no longer fit in the window frames, so Janelle couldn't open the windows, and even though Franklin said he'd fixed it, Janelle was fairly certain there was still mold growing behind the sinks in the bathrooms.

Her sister was anxious to take possession of the building so she could make the repairs herself.

As Olivia expected, Janelle was in the office, sitting at the desk and staring at the computer screen. Olivia polished off the scone and leaned against the doorway. No one could ever mistake her and Janelle as anything but sisters. Janelle was taller and curvier, but they shared the same olive-toned skin and long, shapely legs. They'd both inherited their father's brown eyes and their mother's dark, thick hair. Where Olivia wore her hair long and usually pulled back in a ponytail, Janelle had cut hers in a short and stylish fashion.

There was a time when the two girls had been glued at the hip. Although there was a three-year age difference between them, they had grown up as best friends. Janelle was everything Olivia wanted to be. She was talented, smart, chipper, and gorgeous. Her makeup was always impeccable, and Janelle made even jeans and a chef's coat seem fashionable.

After high school, things had changed. Olivia had realized that she wasn't Janelle. Not even close. Janelle was perfect. She'd married her first boyfriend, and had a wonderful marriage and a successful business. She had a great relationship with both of their parents, and she was even close with their mom's boyfriend.

Olivia, on the other hand, butted heads with her mother and barely saw their father. Until Andrew came along, she changed boyfriends every few months, and she had better relationships with the dogs than the people in town. She was happy in yoga pants and t-shirts, and a good day for her was when she didn't poke herself in the eye with the mascara wand.

When she realized that she'd never be like her sister, something changed.

She and Janelle still had lunch and talked, but something was different between them, and they both knew it.

Neither one of them wanted to admit it.

It was almost ironic that the perfect sister was the one who needed help, but Janelle thought she was doing Olivia a solid. She thought she was coming to Olivia's rescue by offering her this great office space, and maybe that was what was bothering Olivia. Janelle couldn't admit that she needed help from her imperfect little sister.

"I had two dozen scones in the cooling rack. A lovely round number. When I display them in fifteen minutes, will I still have two dozen?" Janelle asked without looking up.

Olivia smiled. "One of them looked a little burnt, and I know how you feel about your scones. Nothing less than perfection will do."

"We don't burn anything in this bakery," Janelle grumbled as she looked up, a dusting of flour in her hair and a sour look on her face. "I'm not having a great morning, Olivia. Yvette was supposed to come by and pick up baked goods an hour ago, but I haven't seen her, and she isn't answering her phone. She's supposed to come by every morning to grab fresh goods. I won't have her selling stale products. My name is on the boxes!"

Olivia cringed. "Janelle . . ."

"And this deal with the brownstone is making me anxious."

Cocking her head, Olivia studied her sister. Was this the break that she'd been looking for? "Are you having second thoughts?" she asked. "Because it's okay if you want to spend more time thinking about this. This is a big decision."

"Second thoughts?" Janelle asked, obviously startled. "Of course I'm not having second thoughts. This is everything that I want. I've been renting for years, but I need to buy. I need to put down roots. I need my customers to know that Happy Endings is here to stay—and you need a home for your business. Franklin has made it clear that it's now or never, so I can't let this opportunity slip through my fingers—but every time I turn around, there's more hoops to jump through. I still need your tax information from last year so I can take that to the bank. Think you can get the paperwork to me by tomorrow? I'm trying to get to the bank by Monday. The pipes are still creaking, and Franklin won't look into it. I need to finalize the sale and get them fixed before they break and flood the place."

I need? Didn't she mean *we* need?

Olivia's heart started to pound in her chest, and she cleared her throat. Tomorrow was too soon. Olivia wasn't ready. "Janelle, Yvette is dead."

There was a moment of silence before Janelle pushed her chair back and stared at Olivia. "What?" she asked softly.

"Andrew and I were out walking the dogs when I spotted her food truck. She was murdered sometime this morning."

"Murdered!" Janelle's eyes widened. "What happened?"

Olivia hesitated. She wasn't sure how much she should discuss about the case when Nick hadn't even processed the scene, but this was her sister. "I think someone drowned her in her coffee vat."

"That's not possible," Janelle said, shaking her head. "No one in this town is capable of that."

"She was on the floor and soaked in coffee."

"Soaking in coffee?" Her sister laughed. "Olivia, she probably just spilled coffee on herself. Maybe she had some medical issue that we didn't know about. You've been reading too many mystery books!"

Olivia rolled her eyes in annoyance. "You read those awful

romance books! I don't bring that up whenever you try to get involved with my love life!"

Janelle ignored her. "It wasn't like she'd let people get to know her. Yvette is—was a loner. You'd think someone who served caffeine for a living would have more pep in her step. She was always alone and a little surly."

"She dated Jacob for over a year. She was going to marry him," Olivia protested. She wasn't sure why she was coming to Yvette's defense. The truth was, Yvette always did have an attitude.

"She literally left him at the altar. Maybe if she'd married him and put down some roots, she would have been happier."

Olivia frowned. It wasn't like Janelle to be so judgmental. "You don't know that Yvette would have made a good wife for Jacob."

"Speaking of Jacob, we also need to sign the paperwork for Franklin," Janelle said as she reached across her desk.

Franklin was Jacob's father, but it wasn't the smoothest segue. Watching Janelle reach for the papers made Olivia panic just a little, and she quickly tried to distract her sister.

"Well, Jacob seems very happy with Samantha, and I'm sure they'll be getting married anytime now," she babbled. "Do you and Patrick have plans tonight?"

"No," Janelle said with a frown before her eyes brightened. "But you do. What are you wearing tonight?"

Happy that they weren't talking about the building anymore, Olivia relaxed. "What am I wearing tonight? Why?"

"Andrew is taking you to a fancy dinner. What are you wearing? I'll be happy to loan you a dress."

Wait, what? Olivia narrowed her eyes. "How do you know about the dinner? Andrew just told me about it an hour ago." Her suspicions were confirmed when Janelle's eyes widened and she started tapping her fingers on the desk. Her sister was a horrible liar, and Olivia recognized the signs. Andrew *had* told Janelle about the dinner.

"We were just talking last night, and he mentioned it," Janelle said uneasily.

Crossing her arms, Olivia cocked her head. "Except that Andrew was with me last night, so if he spoke to you, it was over the phone. Why would Andrew call you?"

The tapping got louder. "He didn't call me. I called him. I mean, I called you. I had a question for you, but Andrew picked up the phone and answered the question, so I didn't need to talk to you."

There were so many holes in that story that Olivia couldn't even figure out which to point out first, but she felt bad for Janelle and let it go. It didn't really matter. It just confirmed what she already

31

knew. "I've got some clients to take care of tonight."

"I'll walk them. You deserve a nice night with Andrew."

"You hate dogs."

"I don't hate dogs."

"You hate walking the dogs."

"I don't hate walking the dogs. Go have dinner with Andrew. He already made the reservations. Stop by the house and pick a dress before you go home today. Actually, don't do that. You'll pick something inappropriate. Take the green halter dress and pair it with the silver teardrop earrings. You'll look amazing."

Olivia had opened her mouth to argue with Janelle when there was a knock at the door. She turned and was surprised to find the sheriff standing in the doorway. "Nick! Finished processing the scene already? What did you find?"

He sighed. "Olivia, I asked you not to talk about it with anyone."

"It's just Janelle, and I didn't go in detail!" she protested.

Nick looked resigned as he shook his head. "My deputies are still looking everything over."

"Did you look at the surveillance camera?"

"I did," he said quietly. "That's why I'm here."

Not understanding, Olivia shook her head. "You need to talk with me about the camera? I promise that I didn't touch or fiddle with it."

"No. I'm here to talk to your sister."

"Janelle?" Olivia turned her head and saw that her sister had gone pale. "Janelle, what's going on? Why does Nick want to talk to you about Yvette's surveillance camera?"

"I saw Yvette this morning," she said weakly, and stood up. "But I didn't kill her."

Nick's face remained impassive as he nodded his head. "I just need you to come to the station and answer a couple of questions."

Shocked, Olivia stared at her sister. Why hadn't she said something when they were talking about Yvette? "Okay, well, I'm coming with you."

"No, it's fine," Janelle said, but her voice shook just a little, and as she took a step, she looked like she might fall over at any minute.

"It's not fine," Olivia snapped. "I don't know what's going on, but you're not going alone."

"Olivia, you can come to the station, but I can't let you in the interrogation room," Nick said softly. "Policy."

"Interrogation room?" Janelle repeated. "A couple of questions just turned into an interrogation. Do I need a lawyer?"

"That's up to you," Nick said, even more quietly.

Janelle reached out and squeezed Olivia's hand.

"It's okay," Olivia whispered. "You didn't kill Yvette. We're just going to go, and you'll answer his questions, and it'll be all over. If it gets intense, we'll have Patrick get a lawyer. There's nothing to worry about."

"Right." Janelle nodded her head. "Nothing to worry about."

Privately, Olivia didn't agree. Unless they could prove that Janelle wasn't the last person to see Yvette alive, her sister was going to be in big trouble.

CHAPTER FOUR

In the chaos of accompanying Janelle to the sheriff's station, Olivia had left her phone at Happy Endings. The interrogation had taken much longer than anticipated, and, not trusting Janelle to actually walk the dogs, Olivia did her final round early so she could have time to prepare for her dinner date. Of course, that didn't stop Lily, the dachshund, from breaking free and chasing after a squirrel or Goodwin from tearing down the shower curtain while she was trying to shower and get ready. It wasn't until she was on her way to Janelle's to get the dress that she realized she was already fifteen minutes late to dinner.

So she showed up at L'Amore dressed in yoga pants and a tank top that said *If I'm running, please call the cops. Someone is chasing me.* She could tell that the hostess, a young, buxom blonde in a ridiculously low-cut black dress, was about to turn her away, when Olivia saw Andrew and rushed past her with a hurried apology.

The blonde was showing way too much cleavage to judge Olivia's outfit, anyway.

Andrew, on the other hand, looked better than good. Dressed in a gorgeous dark suit with a light blue shirt and the striped tie that she'd given him last month for his birthday, he absently swept his hand through his dark, shaggy hair, wearing the most patient expression while he popped something in his mouth.

Twenty-five minutes late. She was twenty-five minutes late, she hadn't been able to call him, and he was still patiently waiting for her while looking like the cover of *GQ*.

He was perfect. It was almost unfair how perfect he was.

When he raised his eyes, shock registered on his face, and she struggled for words. "I'm sorry. Andrew, I'm so sorry."

"I was starting to think that you stood me up," he said slowly as he stood and kissed her cheek. "I was hoping to see you in a sexy dress, but it's just like you to surprise me."

His calm was almost annoying. He should have been outraged! It was almost like he didn't care. "I would never stand you up on purpose! I left my phone at Happy Endings when Nick picked Janelle up to question her, and then the dogs were running rampant, and I was on my way to Janelle's to change because she said I could borrow a dress, probably to avoid a situation where I showed up wearing something highly inappropriate like what I have on, but I realized how late I was, and I am so sorry." She took a deep breath and waited to see how he would react.

He blinked and frowned. "I'm just glad that you're here," he said slowly, giving an obviously all-purpose response. She knew she'd spoken quickly . . . but then comprehension dawned on his face. "Wait—did you just say that Nick questioned Janelle?"

Olivia opened her mouth to explain the horrible afternoon, and then she saw the champagne bucket next to the table. Her eyes went to the half-eaten stuffed mushrooms on the table, and her thoughts raced. Andrew rarely drank champagne. Did he think it would pair well with the mushrooms? Did he want a celebratory drink if she said yes to his proposal?

When she said yes. Because of course she would say yes. Andrew Patterson was the perfect man, and for some unknown reason, he loved her. He was patient with her. He was handsome. He was smart and stable, and Lord, could that man kiss. Any woman would be lucky to marry him.

She'd shown up twenty-five minutes late to the proposal. She was dressed in workout gear at a five-star French restaurant. She had ruined everything. Surely he wouldn't propose now, would he?

As her eyes swept the room, she realized that everyone was staring. Amidst the white tablecloths and long-stemmed candles, the classy dresses and tailored suits, she stood out like a sore thumb. Tugging nervously on her ponytail, she met their disapproving glares with a haughty expression. She didn't owe them an explanation!

"Olivia? You're staring at the champagne bottle. Did you want me to pour you a glass?" he asked softly.

Blinking, she raised her eyes and smiled weakly. "No! I wasn't staring at the champagne. I was staring at . . ." Her voice trailed off when she saw the couple in the corner. "Jacob."

"Jacob?" Andrew turned his head, and Olivia grabbed his hand in alarm.

"No! Don't look," she hissed.

"If I wasn't so comfortable in this relationship, I might be concerned that you're staring at another man," he teased. "Jacob and Yvette used to be engaged, right? She broke off the engagement."

Olivia shook her head and spoke in a hushed tone. "Sometimes I forget that you didn't grow up here. Jacob and Samantha were high school sweethearts. They were together all through college, and when they broke up, the whole town was stunned. You should have heard the gossip. It was even more shocking when Jacob and Yvette started dating. We all thought she was just a rebound, but they were together for a whole *year*. He actually proposed, and it wasn't because Yvette was pregnant. She didn't just break off the engagement. She never showed up to the wedding. Yvette abandoned him at the altar. It was, like, the biggest scandal of the year. Of the decade!"

"Ouch." Andrew grimaced. "Poor guy."

"Yeah. It was rough, but he and Samantha got back together, and there doesn't seem to be any bad blood. Jacob actually looks sad that Yvette is gone."

"That surprises you?" Andrew asked softly. "He asked her to marry him. He loved her, and he thought that he'd spend the rest of his life with her, and now she's dead. Which brings me back to what Nick was doing with Janelle today."

Sitting across from Jacob, Samantha turned her head and glared at Olivia. In high school, they had never been close. Samantha was blonde and leggy, with perfect features and a ridiculously thick fringe of lashes framing her beautiful green eyes. She had been the popular cheerleader, and Olivia had been the equivalent of a band geek. Except that their high school was too small to have a marching band.

Samantha had never been one to keep her displeasure to herself, and she continued to shoot Olivia dirty looks. Ashamed of being caught staring, Olivia averted her gaze and shook her head.

"Janelle was on the security footage. According to the camera, she was the last person to see Yvette alive—which is ridiculous. The killer could have snuck in from the front of the truck on the other side and left the same way—but it doesn't look good. They were arguing outside. Heatedly. Their fight continued in the truck, and Janelle was the only one who came out. Yvette was never seen on the camera again. Janelle said that they were arguing about the baked goods. Yvette's been selling leftover scones and muffins, and it upset Janelle. She swears that they came to an agreement, and she left."

Andrew looked puzzled. "You don't believe her?"

Her defenses immediately rose. "Excuse me? Of course I believe her! Janelle may be passionate about her business and slightly overprotective of her scones, but she is not a killer!"

Andrew chuckled. "No, she's not. But you look worried." He pushed the appetizer plate over to her, and Olivia popped a mushroom in her mouth. It was so good that she almost moaned before she remembered where they were. Expensive restaurant. Perfect proposal atmosphere. She had to remember to keep Andrew distracted.

"Janelle was in the truck. She touched things. Her fingerprints are going to be all over that crime scene, and even if Nick does believe her, he has to follow the evidence. Right now, the evidence probably points to Janelle. What are we going to do?"

Taking her hand, Andrew gestured to the waiter with his free hand. "We're going to get the check, go home, and figure out a way to relax." He repeated the request to the waiter, who gave Olivia a dirty look before nodding.

"I don't think he likes my outfit," she said with a tentative smile.

Andrew leaned back and shook his head. His eyes roamed over her, and she felt a blush creep up from her neck to her cheeks.

"Probably not, but I certainly do. I love the way those pants cling to your hips."

He was trying to make her feel better, and it only made her feel guiltier. "I ruined your dinner," she said softly. "I'm sorry."

"You didn't ruin anything. After seeing Yvette this morning, I should have postponed the dinner. Even if Janelle wasn't all tangled up in this, seeing Yvette must have upset you."

It hadn't upset her as much as it should have, and she had only her books to blame for that.

He paid the check while their waiter wrapped up the unopened bottle of champagne for them to take home. Settling his hand on her waist, Andrew gently guided her out.

Every time he touched her, she still felt a little thrill. A year of dating, and she still got the butterflies whenever she was around him. You weren't supposed to marry the man who gave you butterflies. You married the man once the butterflies were gone, and you felt safe and secure.

"No point in letting a perfectly good bottle go to waste," he said, his grin mischievous. Olivia watched in disbelief as he popped the cork right there on the sidewalk. "Want to go for a walk and help me drink this?"

Unable to help herself, she laughed and reached for the bottle.

41

"Walk around drinking a bottle of champagne? We'll be the talk of the town tomorrow morning."

"That never stopped you before."

"And it's not stopping me now." Taking a swig from the bottle, she sniffed—the bubbles tickled her nose—and nestled under his arm. "Can we walk to Happy Endings? I left my phone there."

"Sounds like a plan."

"What do we do about Janelle?"

"Olivia, you promised."

"What? What!" She pulled back and stared at him. "It's my sister. I can't let her go to jail."

"She's innocent, Olivia. She's not going to jail. This isn't like one of your mystery books. Nick is not going to put an innocent woman behind bars."

"I'm not saying this is like a book. I'm simply pointing out that someone I love is in trouble. I want to help, Andrew. I would think that you'd want to help, too."

He grabbed her elbow and forced her to stop walking. "Olivia, we're not going to fight about this. Of course I don't want anything bad to happen to Janelle, but I also don't want anything bad to happen to *you*."

She glared at him stubbornly. "I don't want anything bad to happen to me, either," she grumbled. "But I also don't *plan* on letting anything bad happen to me. We can figure out a way to exonerate Janelle without getting involved ourselves. There has to be a way!"

"No." Andrew narrowed his eyes and set his jaw. "If it comes to it, we'll hire a lawyer. That's what normal people do in this kind of situation. I know that you want to help, but you're not qualified."

"Because I'm just a dog walker?" she snapped. "Just because I'm not some hot-shot computer whiz with a master's degree doesn't mean that I'm not smart. I have a college degree in business!" Now was not the time to point out that she'd waffled between a few degrees and only settled on business so she could graduate on time.

"Because you're not a detective. Stop trying to pick a fight with me."

Under his steady gaze, her shoulders slumped. She *was* trying to pick a fight with him, but it felt better than doing nothing. He wasn't wrong, but Janelle was her sister. Even though they didn't always get along, she loved Janelle, and she couldn't just stand by and let her go to jail. "You're right," she admitted finally. "I'm sorry."

"Promise me that you're not going to get involved."

"I already promised you that."

Andrew half-smiled and reached out to tuck a strand of Olivia's hair behind her ear. "I know, but I feel like maybe you've forgotten, now that Janelle is in trouble."

"I haven't. That's why I came to you with this problem. I could have just kept it to myself and acted on my own." Olivia knew that she was pushing the envelope, but she didn't want Andrew to think that he'd completely won. She wasn't about to make that promise again.

Especially if she wasn't able to keep it.

Rose Palmer never had this problem, but she also had a new lover in every book. Olivia was not jealous of that particular detail.

Taking another swig of the champagne, she tried to relax. It was that simple, right? Janelle was innocent. Everything would be fine.

Andrew wrapped an arm around her waist and gently pulled her down the street toward the bakery as they passed the bottle back and forth like a couple of teenagers. Janelle's manager had locked up a few hours ago, but Olivia had a key to the back door. After all, Olivia was soon about to own fifty percent of the building. Why shouldn't she have a key?

Just another thing for her to worry about.

"See if there are any muffins left over," Olivia said as she headed to the office. "We'll snag some since we skipped dinner."

"And have Janelle come after me?" he muttered. "No, thank you."

"Wimp," Olivia teased as she handed him the champagne bottle. Turning on the lamp, she swiped the phone from the desk and paused, her hand hovering over the paperwork from the bank. She should just sign it and be done with it, but the devil on her shoulder was always louder than the angel.

"She should be more concerned about her innocence than the sale, anyway," Olivia muttered as she snagged the papers and shoved them in her purse. If Janelle thought that she'd misplaced them, she'd have to get more copies from the bank, and that would give Olivia just a little more time to think. "I'm the worst."

Andrew loosened his tie as he leaned against the doorjamb with a box in his hands and a guilty look on his face. "Are you sure she won't get mad?"

"Oh, she'll be furious—but we could always smash in a window and blame it on a robber," Olivia said as she cracked the top open and peered inside. "Are those the lemon ones? They're my favorite."

Andrew closed the cover with a decisive gesture, nearly trapping Olivia's fingers, tucked the box in one arm, put a firm hand on her back, and guided her toward the door. "We are *not* breaking a window, and I *know* the lemon ones are your favorite. Hopefully they'll keep you busy so you don't steal my apple pie muffins."

Olivia gasped. "There were apple pie muffins left over? Those are my favorites, too!"

"If you're nice to me tonight, maybe I'll let you have one!"

"Let me have one?" Olivia said in mock indignation as she relocked the bakery. "It was my idea to steal them."

"True, but I actually did the stealing. I'm taking all the risk here!" He handed her the champagne bottle and held a lemon muffin before her face. Sinking her teeth in, she giggled when crumbs fell down her chin.

Andrew pulled the muffin away and polished off the rest in two bites. He moaned in mock ecstasy. "Forget L'Amore. This is the perfect evening."

"Champagne and baked goods? I could not agree more!"

He walked her back to her house. She rented, and it was almost more than she could afford, but she loved the small two-bedroom house. The neighborhood backed up to a small running trail and creek, and each house had its own charming personality. The brick house with its black roof and shutters wasn't what caught her attention, but the bright blue front door had been its selling point.

She kept the small front yard simple and manicured, but she let the back yard grow wild.

Climbing up the brick steps, he stopped her before she could unlock the door. "This night did not turn out the way that I wanted," he whispered as he leaned in and kissed her. It curled her all the way to her toes, and she sighed. "But it was still perfect."

"It doesn't have to be over," she whispered. "You could come in."

Andrew grinned as he kissed her. "So tempting, but it's a beautiful night, and we still have half a bottle of champagne to drink. Why don't you grab Goodwin, and we'll enjoy tonight for a little longer?"

"And then?" she asked, eyebrow raised.

"And then we'll enjoy the rest of our evening inside," he said with a laugh.

"Now that sounds like an excellent plan." For a moment, she forgot all about Janelle and Yvette. He was right. It was a beautiful night. The stars were twinkling bright in the skies above, and there was a warm breeze. Kissing him one last time, she headed inside and leashed her monstrous mutt. "I haven't forgotten about the shower curtain," she said, eyeing him.

He jumped up and kissed her.

"Fine," she grumbled. "I still love you."

Leaving the muffins on the counter, she leashed Goodwin and rejoined Andrew. Goodwin kept his head to the ground and sniffed everything excitedly. She'd adopted him two years ago at a particularly low point in her life. Her previous boyfriend had left her, and her family simply couldn't understand why yet another relationship hadn't worked out. In retaliation, Olivia had decided to get herself a companion that wouldn't judge her. She'd felt a connection with Goodwin the moment she'd met him, even though she'd had no idea about his background. The pet adoption agency had said that someone had brought him in from the streets. It was clear that he'd been loved before, but the owner had never been found. He'd always been a joyful dog, and for Olivia, he came into her life at the perfect time. She'd been between boyfriends and had sworn off men forever.

Until Goodwin found Andrew Patterson. The mangy mutt had broken free of his leash one day and ran straight to the gorgeous stranger walking down the street, even though he knew she'd sworn off men. She'd told him so, often enough.

One thing she could say about Andrew, he didn't give up until he got what he wanted. It had taken him a good three months to finally convince her to go on a date with him. Since then, he'd steamrolled right over her trust issues and neurotic tendencies. He patiently held her hand while she broke up with him three times

48

during the first month. He kissed her when she freaked out over still being with him after six months. He didn't dump her when she refused to move in with him.

As he was the new blood in town, all the eligible women panted after him, but he only seemed to have eyes for her. She looked up and felt her heart flutter.

He flashed her an amused smile. "Are you feeling more relaxed?"

She could have melted against him, but Goodwin pulled on the leash, and she sighed. He was sniffing around a for-sale sign.

"That's Franklin Kennedy's home. Is he moving?"

"Huh. I guess so."

"He's selling the brownstone . . . Now he's selling his house. What's going on?"

Andrew shook his head. "I don't know, but you'd think that if the man was moving, everyone would know about it."

"Darla rents from him. So does Phillip Jackson. Yvette's food truck belongs to him. Do you think he's selling everything?"

"I don't know, babe. Franklin and I don't cross paths much. You can always ask when you sign the paperwork for the brownstone."

Her gut clenched, and she swallowed hard. "Yeah. Sure."

"For the record, I think it's great that you're finally getting an office for your business. It's made me nervous that you're so mobile. You rent rather than own. You work out of your home. I might wake up one day and fine you gone." His tone was teasing, but Olivia could sense the grain of truth in his words, "This office means you'll have roots."

Roots. Right. That seemed to be the word of the week. "You're hogging the champagne," she said with a high-pitched laugh as she grabbed it. At this rate, she was going to develop an ulcer before she signed anything.

She drained the rest of the bottle and moaned as she handed it back to him. "I don't suppose that you have another one of these hiding on your person somewhere."

"You're welcome to check," he said in a husky voice. She didn't know whether it was his tone or the champagne, but she was instantly warmed.

They walked out of the neighborhood and back to Main Street. As they strolled through the park, she paused for a moment to take in the scenery. The crescent moon hung low and could only be seen through a clearing in the trees. It was breathtaking.

She disposed of the champagne bottle in the trash can and turned around to take Andrew's hand again. He was staring at the moon as he ran his hand over his pockets.

Oh, God. Was he searching for a ring? She'd ruined the dinner, but here they were, in a beautiful clearing in the park with a perfect view of the most gorgeous sky. If she were the type of woman who dreamed of a picturesque proposal, this would be it.

Except that she wasn't the type of woman who dreamed of proposals. Or weddings. Or perfect men.

Her breath caught in her throat. What was wrong with her? She loved him. She loved the way his arms wrapped around her protectively at night. She loved the way he calmed her down when she grew anxious. She loved the way he always asked how her day was—and actually listened.

And he loved her. There wasn't a single doubt in her mind that he was the man for her. But marriage? Was she ready for that?

"Olivia," he said softly.

As if the dog sensed her hesitation, Goodwin barked and broke away. "Seriously? I'm the worst dog walker ever," she muttered, and took off after him. "Goodwin! You get back here!"

The dog bounded down the street, his leash trailing behind him. She raced after him. Andrew's footsteps weren't far behind.

The ridiculous mutt ignored all her commands and flew through the square until they reached the caution tape surrounding the food truck. Olivia drew up short when Goodwin ran under the tape and started nosing the ground on the other side.

"Olivia, you can't go under there," Andrew commanded.

"I know that," she snapped, but she ducked under the tape anyway. "Goodwin, stay!"

Her dog was still nosing the ground when Olivia grabbed the leash. She was just about to pull the dog away when she realized what he was doing.

He was licking up crumbs. "Andrew, hold him for a second," she said as she pulled Goodwin away and handed him the leash.

"What? Olivia, you're going to get in trouble."

"There's something here," she muttered as she ignored him. Pulling out her cellphone, she turned on the flashlight and studied the ground. "Crumbs. Andrew, these are the missing scones."

"That's great. We can call Nick after you get back on the right side of the tape."

"Janelle was right. Yvette was selling stale baked goods. If the killer was eating fresh scones when he left, it wouldn't have crumbled like this."

"That's not really helping Janelle's case," he pointed out tightly.

"When Janelle left the food truck this morning, she would have walked directly to her shop. She has no reason to walk in this direction. She doesn't live that way. She doesn't work over there. This could exonerate her!"

Her boyfriend didn't respond, and she turned her head. He was staring at the tree line, and she sighed. God, was he staring at the moon? Was he going to propose now? They were talking about her sister's innocence! "It might," he called out in a curious voice.

Taking a quick picture of the crumbs, she carefully backed away from the crime scene. "What are you staring at?"

With a strange smile, he pointed to the trees. "What do you see?"

"The moon is pretty, Andrew, but that's hardly the most pressing issue here."

"Not the moon, baby."

Confused, she realized that he was pointing at the trees. It wasn't until she concentrated that she saw the steadily blinking red light. "It's a camera," she whispered.

"It's a camera," he agreed.

"It's so well hidden. No one would ever see it in the daytime. It's farther away. It's got a wider angle, and it's hidden. The killer wouldn't have known about it. Andrew, this could clear Janelle!"

"Call Nick," he said with a gorgeous smile.

In that moment, Olivia would have said yes to anything he asked of her. Pulling out her phone, she called the sheriff.

CHAPTER FIVE

Pacing nervously, Olivia stared at her phone. Janelle was meeting with Nick, and the sheriff had refused to talk to Olivia ahead of time.

Doubts flashed in her mind. She and Nick were friends. She covered for him when his wife thought he was out walking the dogs and getting exercise. If it were good news, he would have told her. Why would he keep things from her?

Janelle wasn't a killer, but what if there was something wrong with the camera? What if it was turned off during the murder? What if she'd made things worse?

"Status quo," she whispered. "I should have just left things alone. I just made things worse. What have I done?"

The phone interrupted her panic attack, and she grabbed at it so quickly that it fell to the floor. "No. Janelle! I'm here," she yelled at the still-ringing phone, for all the good it would do. She picked it up and answered. "I'm here!"

"Hi," her sister said, laughing joyfully. "You sound so panicked!"

"Don't play with me," Olivia snapped. "What did Nick say?"

"You did good, little sister. You did good."

Relieved, Olivia sank against the wall. "Oh, thank God. So who did it?"

"It shows Yvette waving goodbye to me as I left, but it didn't show anyone else until you and Andrew showed up. The lens was zoomed in on the truck. If the killer came in from the front and stayed behind the truck, the video wouldn't have caught it. So it doesn't solve the whole case, but it does exonerate me."

"That's great," Olivia said as she straightened. "I'm glad that I could help."

"So you'll come by tomorrow and sign the paperwork for the bank?"

She was saved from answering by the beeping of her phone. Thankful for the distraction, she glanced down to read the text and laughed. "Mayor Henderson is calling for a town meeting!"

"Already? Didn't we just have one this quarter?"

"Someone just got murdered, Janelle. I don't think that they want to talk about curb appeal and raising HOA fees," Olivia said dryly. "It's tonight at five. You want to go?"

"Not especially. It always just turns into some ridiculous fight."

Olivia grinned. "I know. That's why they're so fantastic! C'mon. We'll go to the meeting and we'll have dinner at End Game afterward."

Janelle sniffed. "I don't know about End Game, but I guess I could meet you there. Patrick has a meeting tonight, so I was just going to spend a few extra hours at Happy Endings."

Olivia was pleased. It had been a long time since she and Janelle had hung out together. Lately, they'd just gotten together to talk about the bank loan or her love life. Maybe this was exactly what she needed. She'd start to see Janelle as her sister again, rather than this uptight stranger her sister had turned into.

Maybe then she'd feel more comfortable going into business with her.

Olivia didn't bother changing out of her dog-walking clothes. She'd grown up in Lexingburg, and the town no longer had high expectations of her. There was a time when everyone had thought the Rickard girls were just the darlings of the town. Everyone still thought that of Janelle.

Olivia . . . not so much.

It wasn't that she was a troublemaker, and it wasn't that she just didn't have much motivation or aspiration. It was just that all of Olivia's best-laid plans usually went awry.

I'm not that girl anymore, she reminded herself. She had a successful business. She had a great boyfriend. No one made bets about the next heart she'd break or the next job venture that would fail.

It wasn't her fault that she hadn't realized she didn't have a green thumb until she'd tried to work for the flower shop. She did know that customer service wasn't really her thing, but Janelle had insisted that she wait tables at the new cafe a few years ago. The reception position had seemed like a solid fit—until her boss had decided that her legs were touchable.

The dog-walking thing worked. For a solid year, she'd never had a lag in business. And despite what Nick thought, she wasn't all *that* nosey.

Still, no one blinked an eye when she showed up at the town hall wearing yoga pants and a shirt that read *Exercise . . . Eggs are Sides.*

The meetings were a notorious waste of time. The mayor generally had an inflated sense of his own importance and often used the meetings to boast about his ludicrous accomplishments—like planting flowers on the side of the road. Unfortunately, as a business owner, Olivia was required to come to the meetings on the off chance that the mayor was about to push an agenda that would affect her business. Mostly, the meetings turned into an inane circus affair with one business entrepreneur yelling at another for something ridiculous, like competitive pricing. Last time they'd met, the owner of the vintage clothing store was angry because the kids' clothing store next door was too rowdy. The verbal argument had escalated into a screaming match better than any toddler's temper tantrum.

Today, the town hall was packed with people curious about the murder. Olivia's neighbor, old man Cramer, hobbled up and gave Goodwin some love but ignored her. Delilah Devereux, the owner of Delilah Silks, gave her a nasty look, but everyone else was friendly enough. Lady Celeste waved excitedly to her, but Olivia ducked her greeting and found a seat next to Janelle and Olivia's good friend, Jackie Jones.

"Janelle brought treats," Jackie said excitedly, passing over a cookie. She was a small woman sporting glasses and fiery red hair. She owned Shelfie, and for a while, everyone had written her off as a mousey bookworm. Olivia knew she had a hot temper and little patience, but it wasn't until the town had revolted against Jackie's erotica section that people had gotten a taste of her temper.

Jackie had won that round, and she gleefully told Olivia whenever one of her protesters sneaked in to buy the newest hot read.

"Thanks, Janelle," Olivia said as she snatched a cookie. "Double-fudge chocolate chip? How am I not a thousand pounds by now?"

"It's all that exercising that you do," Jackie said with a grin.

"I would hardly call strolling around town with a bunch of dogs *exercise*. Old Man Cramer walks faster than you," Janelle sniffed.

Olivia shrugged. "That's when they behave. I burn all the calories chasing after them when they break free."

"You are the worst dog walker ever!" Jackie reached across and snagged another cookie from the bag. "I'm going to need the sugar high if Donald complains about my window display again."

"Jackie, you literally displayed covers with half-naked men and a sign that said 'cheat on your husband with men who still have their hair,'" Janelle chastised.

The bookshop owner just shrugged. "Just because Donald is bald doesn't mean that he had to take it so personally!"

The man in question, Donald Henderson, walked behind the podium and the whole room went quiet. It was all Olivia could do not to laugh when she saw the blond toupee on the man's head. He hadn't just gotten upset when Jackie had put up her display. He had actually gone out and bought a wig.

"Citizens of Lexingburg!" The man's robust voice boomed in the large meeting room. "I appreciate you all coming here on such short notice. I know by now the rumors that have circulated about young Ms. Dunn's death. I'm here to set the record straight. Earlier today our very own Sheriff Limperos held a national press conference to help calm the public and inform them . . ."

"I'm sorry," Olivia whispered, leaning over to Janelle, "is that pride in his voice? We're talking about a murdered woman!"

60

"You know Mayor Henderson. He's on a warpath to put Lexingburg on the map."

"Maybe he did it," Olivia said in disgust as she leaned back in the folding chair. Tuning out the conference, she tried to channel Rose Palmer's power of observation as she surveyed the town hall. Was the killer here?

There were a few notable absences. Franklin Kennedy, one of the town's more influential members, was missing, as was his son Jacob, Yvette's ex-fiancée. The sheriff himself wasn't there, which surprised Olivia. She had a feeling it wasn't because Donald hadn't tried.

She could just picture the conversation now: the mayor trying to convince Nick that it was important that he be there to speak at the town meeting, and Nick reminding him that it was more important that he catch a killer. That probably pissed Donald off to no end.

Olivia's mom was also missing, and that was really strange. Pamela Rickard had always been a big part of the community. When Olivia's parents had still been together, her mom had been the stereotypical domesticated stay-at-home mother. She organized bake sales, was the PTA president, and even led a Girl Scout troop for a year before she realized that her daughters were not exactly Girl Scout material. When Olivia's parents divorced, Pamela put that leadership experience to good use and took a job teaching, until she worked her way up to assistant principal. She had retired last year and moved in with her long-time boyfriend, Joseph Bunner.

Now that Olivia's mom had all this free time on her hands, she threw herself into the community, and she bullied her daughters into helping her.

Concerned, Olivia leaned over again to whisper to Janelle. "Where is Mom?"

Janelle gave her a strange look. "She's at Dawson Vineyard for a few days with Joseph. She won't be back until tomorrow. She didn't tell you?"

"Maybe," Olivia admitted. She had a bad habit of deleting her mom's voice messages when it sounded like she was about to ask Olivia to help her with yet another bake sale or fundraiser event.

"Ms. Rickard, am I boring you?" Donald asked suddenly. All eyes turned on her, and Olivia gave him her best smile.

"I'm so sorry, Mayor Henderson, I was just trying to comfort Janelle. This whole situation with Yvette has her very upset. You know how close they were," she lied.

"Olivia!" Janelle hissed.

Donald gave her a suspicious look. "As I was saying, Sheriff Limperos has asked if anyone has any information on this horrible crime to call the tip line. Now, before we adjourn, I believe the Lady Celeste has an announcement to make."

Crap. Before Olivia could figure out how to make her escape, Celeste stood. Today she was decked out in a bright blue beaded headscarf with a matching long blue-and-green printed dress. Celeste almost floated to the front of the room and waved her hands around. "Thank you so much, Mayor Henderson. We very much appreciate you putting our minds at ease during this troubled time."

Donald practically beamed as he stepped aside. Almost everyone knew that he had a huge crush on Celeste—everyone except Celeste, although Olivia privately suspected that the alleged psychic did know and used it to get all of her projects approved. If Olivia should hanker to open a pet psychic business, Donald would shoot her down before she could even knock on his door.

"I'm so pleased to announce that dog walker Olivia Rickard and I . . ."

"Oh, no," Olivia moaned. She was going to publically align herself with Olivia.

". . . are teaming up for a special segment . . ."

"Make her stop," Olivia whispered in dread. She tried to sink lower in her chair.

". . . to help this town better communicate with their pets. Next

63

week only, I'll be hosting an open session for you to bring your pets to me and ask those questions that have always plagued you. After that, it will be by appointment only. Olivia, darling, would you like to stand up?"

"Kill me," Olivia pleaded under her breath. "Kill me, right now!"

"Stand up," Janelle said loudly with a grin. "I'm *so* interested in this!"

"You don't even have a pet!" Olivia shot back.

"I might get one!"

"Olivia," Celeste urged.

Slowly standing, Olivia gave the grinning faces of the crowd a sheepish smile. "Lady Celeste approached me yesterday morning about the project," she said awkwardly. "So if that's something that you're into, please let her know."

She tried to sit back down, but Celeste wasn't finished yet. "Olivia, how could the pet owners of Lexingburg benefit from this kind of session?"

"Not a clue," Olivia muttered before Jackie reached over and pinched her. "Ouch. I mean, I can't speak for the cat lovers here, but dog owners might want to know why their dogs like to dig in a certain spot in the yard, or why they bark at the same person over and over again. You all know those funny little quirks."

"Exactly," Celeste said cheerfully. "Olivia, Goodwin, and several of Olivia's other furry clients will be at my shop next Thursday at six o'clock for our very first session."

"I will?"

"I encourage everyone to bring their pooches and come out and join us!"

Celeste sank into a low bow, and Olivia slowly sat back down.

Jackie winked. "Oh, I don't think there's a single one of your clients that would miss that."

Olivia covered her face with her hands. "I hate this town."

CHAPTER SIX

"Andrew, there's someone here to see you. She says she's your fiancée's sister?" Cora, Andrew's secretary, sounded confused as she relayed the message. "I didn't realize that you'd asked Olivia to marry you."

Andrew groaned. "I haven't. You can show her in." Janelle had gotten just a little too excited when Andrew had announced his intentions to propose to Olivia. He could see now that it had been a huge mistake. He knew that proposing to Olivia would take some work. The love of his life didn't make anything easy, but Janelle wasn't proving to be the best sidekick.

Janelle was still wearing her Happy Endings chef coat when she bustled in. "Andrew! I had no idea you had such a nice office! Huge oak desk. Living plants. Plush furniture. I just assumed that you worked in some cramped cubicle."

"I'm the head of the IT department," Andrew explained, eyebrow raised. "You've got some flour right here." Pointing to his right cheek, he watched as Janelle absently swiped at her own face.

"I wanted to personally thank you for turning over the evidence that exonerated me. I just left the town meeting, and it would have been horribly embarrassing if I were still a suspect." She put a basket of muffins on his desk and sat down.

"I would say that Goodwin and Olivia are to thank for that," he said mildly. Janelle had a way of overlooking her younger sister, and while Andrew tried not to get in the middle of it, he knew it bothered Olivia.

Janelle waved her hand to dismiss him. "Right. Anyway, I heard that things didn't go well at L'Amore. I just wanted to say that I'm so sorry. It's just like Olivia to ruin her own proposal dinner."

Andrew cocked his head. "Things didn't work out, but I wouldn't say that it was Olivia's fault. We *did* find that camera because things didn't work out. Besides, I'm not entirely sure that a fancy dinner is the way to go."

"What do you mean? Every woman dreams of a romantic proposal."

He frowned. "I thought Patrick proposed to you in your school's dining hall?"

"Exactly. I love Patrick, but Olivia deserves better than that. It's a miracle that she even found you, and I want this proposal to be perfect for her. What's your next plan?"

Scratching his head, Andrew tried not to look dismayed. The truth was that he hadn't planned anything else. He didn't want the proposal to seem forced. He wanted the question to come naturally because that was when Olivia was more relaxed. At the restaurant, she'd looked like a deer caught in headlights. He'd known it was a mistake the moment he'd asked her to go to dinner with him, but Janelle had been so insistent. The walk home had been the perfect opportunity, but Goodwin had ruined that. "With everything going on in town, I don't know that now is the right time . . ."

"You're stalling," Janelle tapped her foot impatiently. "I know that Olivia felt compelled to help me when Nick suspected me of Yvette's death—and I appreciate her help, but that's all behind us now. Olivia has no other distractions."

"She's about to make a huge purchase," Andrew pointed out.

"Yes, but we've talked about that, and she's fine with it. There's no reason to use that as an excuse."

Privately, Andrew wasn't so sure. One thing he knew about Olivia was that when she was okay with something, she did it. No hesitation. The fact that she hadn't signed the papers was cause for concern. "Still, we both know that Olivia doesn't do well with a lot of change. I think it's best if I just hold off."

"Do you love my sister?" Janelle demanded.

"More than anything."

"And you want to marry her?"

"More than anything."

Janelle stood and shouldered her purse. "Then you need to act on it. You know Olivia's history with men. You need to put a ring on her finger before she decides to move on."

"Olivia's not going anywhere," Andrew said calmly. "But I promise you that I'll give it some thought."

"You do that." When she opened the door, someone was standing in her way. "Excuse me," she said haughtily as she slipped by.

Brett Marco, one of Andrew's employees—and his best friend—gave Janelle a strange look. "My apologies," he said as he stepped aside. Watching her march down the hall, he shook his head. "That has to be Olivia's sister. She's a little terrifying."

"Janelle takes after their mother," Andrew said ruefully. "But she has a good heart."

"I'd heard a rumor that you had a fiancée now. I'd congratulate you, but I'm a little hurt that you didn't tell me yourself."

Andrew rolled his eyes. Cora had a thing for Brett, so she embraced every chance she could to talk to him. "I am thinking of asking Olivia to marry me, but I haven't done it yet. I tried to do it Janelle's way and ask her at L'Amore last night, but things didn't exactly go as planned."

"She turned you down?"

"She was twenty minutes late, showed up in her work clothes, and looked like she wanted to bolt."

Brett grimaced. "Olivia doesn't strike me as the type to enjoy L'Amore. If I were you, I'd propose at End Game."

"End Game?" Andrew stared at him. "You're kidding me."

Shrugging, Brett reached to snag a muffin. "Why not? Olivia is a casual girl, and you both love that place. She's the kind of woman who wants to be in a familiar atmosphere."

"For some reason, I can't imagine telling our kids that I proposed to their mother between bar fights and a home run."

"End Game isn't *that* bad," Brett mumbled, his mouth full. "Trust me, End Game is the way to go. And you've got to give her some space. Let her stew over the distance between you so the proposal is that much more a surprise."

"Why am I taking advice from a single man?"

His friend grinned. "I might be single, my friend, but I know women."

"Get out, and stay away from my muffins!"

Leaning back in his chair, Andrew watched with a wry grin as Brett mockingly threw up his hands in surrender and retreated. His friend wasn't wrong. Even though Brett wasn't into long-term relationships, his women were always happy. Even when things ended, he still managed to stay friends with them. Maybe he really was on to something.

One thing was certain. Andrew knew he couldn't keep taking advice from Janelle.

*   *   *

After the town meeting, Olivia walked back to Main Street with Jackie. "What is wrong with this town? People are actually excited about Lady Celeste's pet psychic week. Someone was murdered here! Shouldn't that be the hot topic?"

"Oh, trust me, people are talking about that as well. Everyone assumes that it was a tourist. No one in Lexingburg would commit murder!"

"Are you kidding me? This town is full of repressed rage." They turned the corner and saw Delilah standing outside of Delilah's Silks with her French poodle, Duchess. "There's a ball of repressed rage right there."

"Olivia!" Jackie laughed. "Delilah isn't so bad."

"I was talking about Duchess. I know *I* would want to kill someone if I was Delilah's pet," Olivia whispered. As they approached the sophisticated woman, Olivia plastered a smile on her face. In high school, Delilah had won all the awards and was prom queen. There was no rivalry between the two because Olivia had been certain Delilah didn't even know Olivia existed. That had changed when Andrew moved into town.

As soon as she'd laid eyes on Andrew, Delilah had pounced. According to Jackie and Janelle, she gave Andrew every opportunity to ask her out, and when he didn't pick up on her blatant signals, she had actually asked him out herself. He had politely turned her down. When Delilah had found out that he was dating Olivia, things turned passively-aggressively ugly. Olivia used to shop at Delilah's Silks, but now, if anything caught her attention, Delilah was quick to whisk it away and let her know that it wasn't for sale. Janelle actually caught Delilah telling people that Olivia didn't really walk the dogs when their owners were at work—completely unfounded, and luckily it didn't hurt Olivia's business, but it was then that Olivia knew that Delilah meant business.

Even though Olivia and Andrew had been going out for a year now, Delilah still flirted shamelessly with Andrew and made no effort to hide her hatred of Olivia.

"Olivia," Delilah said with a smirk. "I had no idea you were having trouble communicating with that nasty mutt of yours. It's a good thing that Lady Celeste is here to help you."

Gritting her teeth, Olivia searched for patience. "I'm just trying to show support for a fellow entrepreneur. You and Duchess should stop by. I'm sure Duchess is dying to say a few things to you."

Jackie snorted. "Excuse me, ladies. I've got to unpack today's delivery."

Olivia wanted to beg Jackie to stay, but she knew how dangerous it was to show weakness in front of Delilah. Already, a cruel smile was curving over the woman's face. "What does Andrew think of your new partnership?"

She opened her mouth to tell Delilah that her relationship with Andrew was none of Delilah's business when her phone rang. Looking down, she privately thanked her boyfriend for his amazing timing. Meeting Delilah's steady gaze, she answered it. "Hello lover boy," she purred.

Delilah sniffed and whirled around. As she stomped off, Olivia heard Andrew clear his throat. "Did you just call me lover boy?"

"Sorry," Olivia admitted. "Delilah was taking shots at me."

"I'm sure that's not true," he murmured. Andrew was a brilliant man—except when it came to Delilah's obsession with him. "How's your day going?"

Olivia rolled her eyes but let the matter drop. "Janelle was cleared."

"I heard. So Nick is going to make an arrest?"

"Unfortunately, no. The camera didn't show anyone else until we showed up. How did you hear about it?"

"So how was Janelle cleared?" Andrew asked, ignoring her question. Olivia heard him mutter something to someone else, and she waited until she had his attention again.

"It showed Yvette waving to her as she left. So Janelle left her alive."

"So maybe Yvette died of natural causes."

She sighed in exasperation. "She drowned in coffee, Andrew. That is not a natural cause."

"Right. Well, at least Janelle isn't involved anymore. Want to join me at End Game for a drink in a little bit? We can celebrate your good work."

All was forgiven with the unexpected compliment. She hadn't thought Andrew would actually support her investigation. "My good work? You were the one who found the camera."

"Yes, I did. I'm talking about you not getting involved."

So much for his support.

Biting her bottom lip, Olivia shook her head. "What time are you leaving the hospital?"

"I'm actually heading out now, but I've got a few errands to run.

I can meet you in an hour."

"What kind of errands?" she asked absently.

"The kind of errands that aren't any of your business," he teased. "See you in an hour?"

Olivia snorted. He wasn't the only one who could tease. "Sweetie, I told you that you don't have to keep dyeing your hair. I like the silvery fox look."

"You wish," he chuckled. "My hair is all natural, and you love it."

"I'll see you in an hour." Shaking her head again, she hung up. End Game was a sports bar, but there was no reason she had to go there smelling like dog. She'd already embarrassed him last night. She owed him at least one decent dinner this week, and there was no danger of him proposing at a bar. At least she could relax and enjoy his company.

An hour later, she traded in her active wear for jeans and a decent button-up shirt. She'd shaved her legs just in case he wanted to spend the night, applied lipstick and mascara, and even wore her hair half-up rather than all the way up. And instead of tennis shoes, she wore flats.

End Game was packed, as usual. There weren't too many bars in Lexingburg and even fewer with big-screen televisions. If

Mayor Henderson ever had his way, there probably wouldn't be any bars at all. The mayor believed that alcohol supported crime. The small, dark restaurant had an oval bar in the middle surrounded by a ring of high-top bars on the lower level. There were booths a few carpeted steps up, and brass railings separated the two levels. The walls were covered in sports memorabilia supporting both the local college and several state teams. Seven screens lit up the walls, but luckily Joe, the owner kept the sound off unless there was a major game on.

It was the first place the women called when they couldn't find their husbands, and the last place a man would go to hide from his wife. Joe had an unspoken rule with his clientele. No family drama in his house.

Andrew whistled as he rose from the table. "You look amazing. Have you been watching those makeup tutorials again?"

"Shh," she whispered, looking around. "You're not supposed to know that. And yes. I learned a new way to contour."

He searched her face quizzically. "I'm not really sure what contouring is, but if that's what you did, it looks great. *You* look great."

Chuckling, she gave him a quick peck on the lips. "I did not contour, and you just won some major points."

"Noted. It's probably going to take forever before the server makes the rounds, so I'm going to grab some drinks from the bar. Do you want a lager or a sangria?"

"Joe will cry if you ask him to make me a sangria again. He thinks it's bad for his image."

Andrew waited patiently. "So are you going to ask me to make Joe cry?"

"You'd do it, too, wouldn't you? That's so sweet! A beer would be great."

Settling back in the booth, she gazed up at the televisions. Several games were going at once, but she couldn't identify any of them. Most of the diners had their eyes glued to the screen. End Game had a lot of regulars, and Andrew, in his suit, didn't really fit in, but he always said that he liked the environment. She had a feeling it was because he missed his brothers and the feeling of testosterone rivalry.

He returned with their drinks, and she tentatively sipped at her beer. It was smooth, and it hit all the right spots. Sighing, she leaned back in the booth and relaxed. "I didn't realize how tense I was about this whole Yvette situation."

"So you're feeling more relaxed? Happy?" he asked intently, watching her over his own beer.

"I am. How was work?"

"I don't want to talk about work." Putting his beer down, he reached across and took her hand. "Do you know when I first fell in love in with you?"

Olivia smirked. "I thought it was love at first sight. You, staring at me while my dog attacked you with slobbering kisses. *That* wasn't when you fell in love with me?"

"I'm serious, Olivia. Four months after we started dating, you tried to break up with me. You were mad because I stayed at work for an extra hour without calling you, and you told me that you weren't the kind of woman who sat by the phone and waited for a man to call her."

She slowly put her beer down and straightened. "I remember that night. You kissed me and apologized and said that I couldn't break up with you because you had tickets for us to see the symphony, and they were non-refundable. And I told you that I was only going to stick it out because I wanted to see the symphony. You did *not* tell me that you loved me."

"No, but I knew that I loved you. I did have to stay an hour late, and I thought every minute about calling you, but I wasn't sure if we were at the point in our relationship when I checked in and told you that I was going to be late. That night, you told me that you'd waited by the phone for me to call, and I knew."

Olivia raised an eyebrow. "I'm sorry. You knew that you loved me because I waited by the phone for you?"

"I knew that I loved you because I couldn't stop thinking about you that night. I knew that I loved you because you were waiting for me when I finally drove to your house. I knew that I loved you because there was so much passion in your eyes when you were yelling at me."

"Well, hell, if I had known that, I would have yelled at you a lot more. You have no idea how much I've held my tongue, but now that I know you think it's sexy . . ." she teased with a grin.

"You're such an easy woman to love, Olivia Rickard. I know that you don't think that, but you're such an amazing woman."

Alarm bells sounded in her head. Her fingers twitched, and she fought the urge to pull her hand away. He wasn't seriously going to propose to her now, was he? At End Game? In the middle of cheap beer and drunken sports fans?

Not sure what else to do, she jerked her arm and sent her beer flying. Andrew jumped up, and the apology was already on the tip of her tongue, but he just gave her a strange look. "It's okay," he said quietly. "I'll get someone to clean this up and get you another beer."

As he walked away, she dabbed at the spill and sighed. "Way to go, Olivia. Your perfect boyfriend is trying to propose to you, and you freak out and spill beer all over him."

Rubbing her temples with her fingers, she smiled sheepishly at the waiter as he came back with a cloth to clean things up. "This is my fault, and I'm so sorry."

"No worries," he said with a shrug. "It happens all the time around here."

"Yes, but I'm not drunk. I'm just an idiot."

"I'm sure it was just an accident. I'll get you another one. What are you drinking?"

"My boyfriend is getting me one. My perfect boyfriend who deserves someone way better than me," she muttered. The waiter's eyes widened, and he dropped the cloth. Stuttering an apology, he made a quick exit, no doubt off to tell everyone else about the crazy woman in the corner booth.

Andrew returned with her beer and a calm expression on his face. She knew he wouldn't say anything about her jerking away from him, and that bothered her more than she wanted to admit. "Here you go. If you spill this one, I'm going to make you drink out of a children's cup," he said easily as he slid into the booth.

"I'm pretty sure that you're not allowed to do that in a bar," she said wryly. Just then, Yvette's face filled the television screen and the whole bar quieted. Olivia leaned across the table to hear better, but Joe was already turning the volume up.

A video of Nick's press release played in the background as the news anchor spoke. "Sheriff Nicholas Limperos announced today that there are several persons of interest in the murder of food truck owner Yvette Dunn, but he has not made any arrests. Dunn was drowned inside her place of business in the early hours of Friday morning. This is the first murder Lexingburg has seen in more than a decade."

The audio for the press release resumed and the bar listened in rapt silence as Nick spoke. "Yvette Dunn was a beloved member of our community, and we are devastated by her loss. We are doing everything that we can to bring her killer to justice. The state police have offered their assistance, and we are utilizing their state-of-the-art forensics lab to process the evidence. I promise that this case has our full attention. It does look like that this is an isolated crime, so I do not want the community to panic."

Andrew shook his head. "Isolated crime or not, I'm glad that you and Janelle are no longer involved. Nick's a good cop. I'm sure this case will be closed quickly, and everyone can rest easy again." He reached inside his jacket, and Olivia's eyes widened.

"Ten years is a long time," she said abruptly. "Ten years without a murder investigation. Nick should use more than the state police's labs. He should use *them* for the investigation."

The waiter stopped by and overheard them speaking. The young man shook his head vehemently. "Nick won't need the state police.

81

Franklin Kennedy probably killed her."

At first, she wasn't even sure she'd heard him correctly. No one in their right mind would accuse the wealthiest and most influential businessman in town of murder. Stunned, Olivia stared at him. "What? Why would you say that?"

"When I'm not waiting tables, I'm also an Uber driver, and I had Franklin in the car a couple of weeks ago. Yvette was suing him for breach of contract. He was on the phone for a good ten to fifteen minutes talking to his lawyers about it. Franklin was livid. Apparently, the lawsuit was keeping him from closing on an exclusive resort community in Florida. Believe me when I tell you that he had nothing nice to say about Yvette."

"Did you tell the police that?" Olivia demanded.

The waiter shrugged. "No. I just figured that the police already knew. Do you want another round?"

Waving the waiter off, Olivia turned her head and stared at Andrew. "Do you think that Franklin's capable of killing?" she said in a low voice.

"Nick will get to the bottom of it," Andrew responded sternly. "You don't need to worry about it."

"Right." Olivia sipped at her beer and tried to push it out of her head. Despite her agreement, she just couldn't enjoy the rest of her evening. Not only was she worried that Janelle's landlord was a murderer, but she could feel the space between her and Andrew widening.

CHAPTER SEVEN

"You were going to propose at End Game?" Janelle shrieked. "What were you thinking?"

Andrew winced and sent a pleading look at Patrick. Janelle had asked Olivia that morning to stop by Happy Endings and pick up the paperwork that she'd forgotten the other day, and when Olivia started to make excuses for why she couldn't go, Andrew offered to pick them up.

He shouldn't have even mentioned the plan at End Game, but it just slipped out, and Janelle was on the warpath.

"Janelle, sweetheart, why don't you get us some bagels with cream cheese? I'm starving," Patrick said calmly.

"Are you siding with him? You can starve to death," Janelle snapped, but she stomped behind the counter to do as he asked.

Andrew shot Patrick a thankful look. "I had no idea this would be so difficult," he muttered.

"Trying to figure women out is exhausting," Janelle's husband agreed. "But on this, I do agree with her. Proposing to Olivia at End Game is not the best idea. Olivia might be a casual woman, but she's not *that* casual."

"It wasn't even my idea. A friend suggested it. Believe me, it'll be the last time I take his advice."

Patrick lifted an eyebrow. "You're not talking about Brett, your single womanizer?"

"Maybe," Andrew admitted with a wince. "But he leaves them happy."

"You need to trust your instincts, Andrew. No one knows Olivia better than you. Not even Janelle. Olivia is a different person with everyone. For me, she's the translator I need to figure out Janelle. For my wife, she's the rebellious little sister who needs to cling to her own ideals. She's one type of daughter for her mom and an even different one with her dad. There are only two people she's actually relaxed around. You."

"And Jackie Jones," Andrew breathed. "Patrick, you're a genius."

"Yes, but you don't need Jackie for this. You can figure out how to do this all on your own. Trust your instincts, buddy."

Privately, Andrew wasn't sure he agreed. Olivia wasn't the type of woman who talked about wedding plans with other women, but it was possible that she might have said something to Jackie.

Janelle returned with the bagels and slapped the folder down on the table. "Tell Olivia to be an adult and get this finished. I'm tired of her losing the paperwork."

"It might be best if you sat down and had a talk with her about it. I feel like maybe you aren't communicating with each other," Andrew said carefully.

"We're communicating just fine. She just needs to forget about Yvette's death and focus on her responsibilities. She's been doing this since she was a kid. The week before she started high school, she tried to convince our parents that she was going to skip school and be a dancer instead. She even had a whole routine planned. Believe me, there isn't a lick of talent in that girl's body when it comes to dancing, but she'll do anything to avoid change," Janelle said with a scowl. Patrick reached in the bag for a bagel, and Janelle smacked his hand. "Those are not for you."

"But I asked for them," he protested.

"You said you wanted bagels. I've got something special for you in the back. Give me a couple of minutes, and I'll bring them out to you," she said with a wink.

Andrew stood with the paperwork under one arm and the bag of bagels in the other hand. He couldn't get Janelle's story out of his head. Was Olivia still focusing on the murder because she was afraid that something was about to change? If she was that upset about buying the three-story brownstone, she really needed to have a talk with Janelle about it. The sooner she stopped worrying about it, the sooner she could relax—and he could propose.

Yvette's murder could not have come at a worse time.

Feeling guilty about his reaction to the food truck owner's untimely demise, he checked the clock. He had a good fifteen minutes before he had to leave for work, and if he hurried, he'd be able to catch Jackie beforehand and ask her a couple of questions and get her thoughts. "Thanks for breakfast, Janelle."

"Has Olivia figured out a way to weasel out of Celeste's pet psychic segment?" Janelle asked as he walked by.

Stopping, he gave her a puzzled look. "I'm sorry. A what?"

"She didn't tell you?" Janelle laughed. "Celeste announced at the town meeting that she's partnered up with Olivia and is going to communicate with the pets of Lexingburg. I believe Goodwin's going to be her first victim."

"I remember Celeste mentioning something the other day about it, but she just wanted Olivia to spread the word. You're telling me that Olivia agreed to this?"

"She did."

Of course she did. That was the kind of woman that Olivia was. A big heart who never wanted to hurt anyone or let them down. Smiling to himself, he pushed the door opened and headed to Shelfie.

It seemed that everything Olivia did simply proved that she was the woman for him.

Jackie was wiping the windows down when Andrew knocked on the door and pointed to the logo on the bakery bag. The redhead's eyes lit up with glee, and she hurriedly unlocked the door. "Are you here to bribe me?" she asked as she snatched the bag.

"What makes you say that?"

"I've been expecting it. C'mon in before Delilah sees you out without Olivia. She'll sink her teeth into you if she gets a hold of you."

"I doubt that." Jackie, Janelle, and Olivia had this idea that Delilah was interested in him, but that was absurd. He'd told Delilah a long time ago that he wasn't interested, and the woman had been nothing but nice and polite to him since then. He couldn't understand Olivia's extreme dislike to the woman.

Perching on the arm of a large orange chair, Jackie pulled out one of the bagels and the accompanying plastic container, tore the lid away from the cream cheese, and swiped the bagel through the soft, creamy topping. When she took a bite, her eyes rolled up and she moaned in appreciation. "This is exactly what I needed."

"Those bagels are not free," Andrew reminded her. "Every time I try to propose to Olivia, she bolts. That means that I should ease off and give her some more time, right? Janelle thinks she's throwing herself into this murder investigation to avoid me. She could really hurt herself."

"You're so sweet—and so naive," Jackie said, brushing crumbs off her shirt. "If you want to wait until Olivia is ready, you're never going to get married. She's ready, but she's not going to know it until she's standing at the altar and staring at her groom."

"So how do I do it? Janelle told me to go the fancy restaurant route, and that fell apart. Brett told me "End Game," and she freaked out and knocked her beer off the table. What's your take on it?"

"Pick a place where she's most comfortable. Olivia loves the outdoors. She spends more than half her day outside. Do it then. Casual atmosphere—but without the fried foods and alcohol stains."

"So I should propose at the dog park?" he asked with a frown.

"Maybe a step up from the dog park."

"Care to elaborate?"

Jackie smiled at him. "Bagels only get you generic ideas. Specific details require cupcakes. Stop overthinking it, Andrew. Just keep the ring on you, and when the moment feels right, take it!"

"Right. Okay, I can do that. Thanks, Jackie." Leaning down, he grabbed the bag of bagels and snatched them away despite her protest. "All you get is one bagel."

"Fine. I was going to check to make sure the coast was clear before you left, but now you're on your own. I hope you don't run into Delilah and Duchess."

"She's a nice woman," Andrew said, rolling his eyes. "And she is not interested in me. You all might be friends if you'd just try to be nice to each other."

"See, you're not from here. If you were from here, you wouldn't say that," Jackie sing-songed.

"Can you do me one more favor, Jackie? Can you remind Olivia not to get even more involved in the murder investigation? If the killer wasn't a drifter, Olivia could seriously be hurt."

Jackie waved her hands. "Relax. No one in Lexingburg would murder Yvette. Now get going before you hit traffic."

Shaking his head, Andrew headed to his car. Despite Jackie's warning, the coast was clear. Things were pretty quiet on Main Street. Janelle always got an early start to do her baking, and Jackie opened early to try and snag Janelle's early rush, but most of the shops wouldn't open for another couple of hours. This moment was the reason that he'd moved to Lexingburg.

Andrew had grown up surrounded by people. He'd known

nothing but crowded sidewalks and traffic. He'd gone to a large university and had spent the majority of his life in crowds. So when he took the job at Lowell Hospital, he could have gotten an apartment in the city—but when he drove through Lexingburg, he fell in love. The next thing he knew, he had a studio apartment that overlooked a lush forest and had neighbors who baked him dinner because they feared he couldn't take care of himself.

The first few weeks of living in Lexingburg felt like a waking dream. When he bumped into someone on the sidewalk, he didn't have to immediately check his back pocket to see if his wallet was still there. When he left his keys in the lock, not five minutes passed before someone was knocking on the door to let him know. Women he'd never even met were showing him pictures of their single daughters, and the newspaper actually wanted to do an article on him.

It was amusing, but when he'd laid eyes on Olivia, his whole world stopped. In that moment, he didn't even realize that a huge dog was trying determinedly to knock him down. He only had eyes for the gorgeous mess of a woman trying desperately to regain control of the situation.

He loved it here. This was where he was supposed to be, and if he didn't blow the next attempt at a proposal, he would have everything he'd ever wanted.

CHAPTER EIGHT

Andrew had managed to use some of his many talents to help take Olivia's mind off the case for a few hours last night, but after he fell asleep next to her, her emotions were in chaos. *Franklin Kennedy.*

He was one of the wealthiest members of Lexingburg, but he was also one of the most well liked. He put his money back into the town, he hosted town events, and he settled town disputes. In fact, the only people who didn't like him were his tenants. His generosity didn't usually extend to them, but he was giving Janelle first crack at the brownstone. For that very reason, Olivia needed to leave well enough alone.

But why was Yvette suing him for breach of contract?

She sneaked out of bed, quietly pulled on a t-shirt, and settled at the desk next to the bed, turning the laptop so the light from the screen wouldn't wake Andrew. Spinning absently in the chair, she pursed her lips and tried to sort through her thoughts.

There was only one law firm in town, but Olivia doubted they had the guts to sue Franklin Kennedy. Yvette probably filed the suit in Lowell. After a quick internet search, Olivia found the record of the lawsuit and the name of the law firm that had filed it, but without Yvette or Franklin's SSN, she couldn't find more details.

Looking over the top of the screen, past the glow of the laptop, she watched Andrew while he slept. Olivia was one of those sleepers who sprawled out diagonally across the bed, stole all the pillows, and either rolled in all the blankets or shoved them on the floor. From the moment she'd brought Goodwin home, she'd let the huge mutt sleep with her. The first time that Andrew had spent the night was like a battle.

When he'd tried to sleep over the next night, she'd laughed hysterically, pushed him out the door, and shut it firmly behind him. The idea that the man wanted to give it another go was absurd to her. Her previous boyfriend had demanded that she choose between him and the dog. Obviously, the dog had won. That Andrew was willing to share his bed with her and the dog was so foreign to her that she didn't even want to entertain the idea. Fortunately for him, he hadn't let the matter go. A few days later, when she spent the night at his place, she woke up to find him on the couch. Embarrassed, she apologized for her nighttime feistiness, and he just kissed her and told her that he needed some earplugs because she snored.

Snored!

Olivia did not snore.

He didn't give up, and slowly, they made it work. They staked out quadrants in the bed. He gave up part of his side of the bed because the traitorous dog liked cuddling with him, and she gave up part of her quadrant because Andrew liked cuddling with her. He wore his earplugs.

And he didn't want her investigating this case.

With a sigh, she closed the laptop. Janelle wasn't in trouble with the police anymore. Olivia had no reason to get involved.

When normal people found dead bodies, they didn't get involved. They might have panic attacks before they called the police. Scream a little. Hyperventilate. They didn't let their dogs jump all over the crime scene. They didn't try to investigate on their own. They let the police handle it.

She was no Rose Palmer. She was just a dog walker trying to avoid two life-altering decisions. This was nothing more than a classic case of transference. She needed to face her problems like an adult.

Except that she couldn't shake the feeling that Yvette was *not* murdered by a drifter. If Franklin Kennedy had murdered her, there was a good chance that he would get away with it because he practically owned the town.

That didn't sit well with Olivia.

Goodwin sensed her distress and left the warm comfort of Andrew's side. Padding over to her, he laid his head in her lap and looked at her with those warm, loving eyes, gleaming in the light coming in through the window from the streetlight out front.

"It's okay, buddy," she whispered as she scratched his ears. "I know things are a little strange right now, but I'm going to figure them out."

As if to prove a point, Goodwin looked back at Andrew. "I know," Olivia said. "I know, but for you, he's just a man who smells good, feeds you, and scratches your belly on demand. It's a little more complicated for me."

It was clear from the look in Goodwin's eye that he didn't understand. Sighing, Olivia stroked his muzzle and stood. After glancing at Andrew's sleeping form, she crept downstairs and sat at the kitchen table. The dog followed her and stretched out in the doorway. The folder with the forms that Janelle wanted her to sign mocked her. Groaning, she pushed the papers off the table and watched them flutter to the floor.

Why did all the important people in her life want all these sudden changes? Happy Endings was great, but Janelle didn't really need to buy the brownstone to keep the business. Whoever bought it would be an idiot not to keep renting to her. Olivia didn't need an office. She was a dog walker. No one seemed to care that she worked out of her small home.

"Everything is fine just the way it is. It's fine!" Turning around, she glared at Goodwin. "And I'm not being nosey. I love this town, and I just want to make sure there isn't a crazy killer on the loose! That's all. I just want to make sure that everything is fine before everything *isn't* fine. And there's nothing wrong with that."

Instead of going back upstairs, she headed for the couch. She put in her ear buds and started to open the audiobook file, but then she hesitated.

With a frown, she chose her music instead.

It took another hour before she finally drifted off to sleep.

*   *   *

When her phone rang the next morning, it jolted her out of a dreamless sleep and sent her sprawling on the floor. Hearing Andrew's special ringtone, she shoved her hair from her face and went digging into the couch cushions for her phone. Her ear buds were tangled up and shoved down her shirt, so she followed the wire until she pulled it out. "Andrew," she said breathlessly when she'd finally pulled the headphone jack out and answered the phone.

"Good morning," he said with a sexy drawl. "I was worried that you wouldn't wake up in time, so I thought I'd call you. You sound out of breath. Were you already awake?"

"No, your call woke me up. I just . . . fell off the couch," she admitted. She couldn't figure out a better way to say that. "You didn't wake me up when you left this morning."

"I figured that if you left the bed and went downstairs last night, then you must have fallen asleep late. I wanted you to sleep until the last possible minute, but you've got dogs to walk this morning." Olivia held her breath and waited for him to ask why she'd slept on the couch. "So, by my count, if you get up now, you'll have just enough time to warm up the breakfast sandwich I made for you and get to that monstrous Rottweiler that someone had the audacity to name Snowball."

"You made me a breakfast sandwich?" she asked softly, with a smile.

"Don't get too excited. It's microwavable bacon."

"You didn't leave me enough time to shower," she pointed out.

"I don't think Snowball will mind."

"True. Thank you. I love you."

"Yes, you do. Now I have to go. The nurses were all given iPads to input their patient information, and I'm pretty sure at least a third of them are going to be broken before lunch."

Olivia chuckled. "Good luck with that. Dinner tonight?"

"Not tonight. I'll call you tomorrow. Have a good day." Before

Olivia could ask what he had planned for the evening, he hung up.

An unsettled feeling bloomed in the pit of her stomach. Yesterday he'd had errands that he didn't want to talk about. Tonight he didn't want to have dinner with her. That wasn't like Andrew.

She heated up the sandwich, changed her clothes, and leashed Goodwin. Tossing everything she needed into her messenger bag, she shoved the sandwich in her mouth and headed to the other side of town.

Snowball was her first stop. The hundred-pound-plus male dog wore a spiked collar bought by his father and was taught to growl on command by his mother, but his true owner was the five-year-old girl who'd named him, so when Olivia unlocked the door and found the friendly beast wearing a giant pink bow, it didn't surprise her.

"No tutu today, Snowball? That's all right. I think the bow is fabulous."

Snowball licked her in agreement and bounded around Goodwin. After Olivia got the dog leashed, she headed to her second stop. The dachshund and Snowball weren't great friends, but Goodwin was a great mediator between the two and loved to act as a buffer. Finally, she made it to her unofficial stop of the morning.

"Sheriff," she said in greeting as she took Tucker's leash.

"Thanks for doing this, Olivia. I just have a lot on my plate with Yvette's death," he said, grabbed his car keys out of his pocket, and headed toward his squad car.

Olivia followed him, trailed by a parade of dogs. "You know, you're going to have to skip lunch at End Game today if you don't walk Tucker like you promised Mary you would," she said with a smile.

He grunted in response. It was an argument they had every time Nick paid her to walk Tucker without Mary knowing. Mary wanted Nick to lose weight. She always complained that his blood pressure and cholesterol levels were too high, and to give Nick credit, he did try. On good days, he swapped out his normal cheeseburger for a salad and walked Tucker, but on bad days, he paid Olivia to exercise the dog and ordered an extra beer at dinner.

"How is the investigation going?" she asked quickly as he opened the car door and slid behind the wheel.

"Olivia, Janelle is no longer a suspect. You don't have to be involved with this case anymore."

Staring down at the leashes, she shrugged. "It's just curiosity. We're friends."

"Olivia," he growled, warning in his voice. "What did I tell you?"

"Did you know about Franklin Kennedy?" she blurted out before she could stop herself. "Did you know that Yvette was suing him?"

Nick looked up, surprise in his eyes, but he covered it quickly. "Olivia, you know that if you have a tip, you call it in. You don't need to tell me directly."

"So you didn't know? Are you going to investigate?"

"I won't need you to walk Tucker tonight. Just lock up when you're finished. Thanks again, Olivia." He slammed the car door, started the engine, and turned away from her, looking behind him to back out of the space.

Upset, Olivia watched Nick drive away. She had seen the stress lines around his eyes, and she knew that the investigation was taking a toll on him, but he wasn't even pleased that she'd told him about Franklin. It was a huge motive. Why wasn't he taking it more seriously?

Blowing out her breath, she shook her head. She'd told him. She'd done her job as a citizen of this town. Now it was time to focus on her job. "Come on, guys. Let's go check out the dog park."

A few minutes later, she was watching Tucker, Goodwin, and

Snowball playing happily in the dog park while Lily ignored them and started digging random holes in the corner. Laughing, Olivia followed behind her and filled in the holes so none of the other dogs fell in and hurt themselves.

When the dogs had tired themselves out, she walked them back to their homes, dropping them off one by one, and started to head back to take a shower. When she passed Franklin's house, she stopped at the for-sale sign and casually removed one of the flyers. It didn't surprise her to see that Franklin was using Kristy, a local realtor. He believed in putting his money back in the community and rarely went outside town for anything.

Where on earth could he be moving? How could he be moving and not tell anyone?

Just then, the front door opened, and Franklin walked out, carrying his suitcase. He was an older man, around Nick's age, but in great shape. He had a handsome face and a pleasant demeanor, but he commanded authority. No one second-guessed Franklin on anything.

He and Mayor Henderson were practically glued at the hip. He and Nick were friends. Was that why Nick had brushed off Olivia's tip? He didn't want to have to investigate his friend for murder?

Goodwin jumped and pulled at the leash. Making a split-second decision, she let the leash go and watched as the dog ran to Franklin and jumped up gleefully. The man stumbled and dropped his suitcase.

"Mr. Kennedy, I'm so sorry!" Olivia gushed as she ran forward. "Gosh, but you know Goodwin. He just loves to greet people."

"It's all right, Olivia. No harm done," he chuckled as he patted the dog and then reached down to collect his things.

"You're lucky it's just Goodwin. I had Snowball and Lily earlier. Plus Tucker. You know how excited Tucker gets—but that's just between us. Mary doesn't know that I walk Tucker sometimes. Nick is just so busy with this case. Can you believe that Yvette was murdered just down the street?" She was almost breathless as the words tumbled out of her mouth. Rose was so suave—she was natural at weaseling information out of people. Clearly, it wasn't as easy as it looked.

"Shocking," Franklin agreed. "This is a good town. It was probably a tourist or some homeless person from the city. I can't imagine that anyone here is a murderer."

Olivia smiled brightly. "That thought does make me feel better," she said, as if truly thankful for Franklin's insight. "But Yvette didn't have a lot of friends."

"She could be a difficult person," he admitted with a rueful smile. "But I just can't imagine that anyone who knew her would murder her!"

"Yeah," Olivia said, nodding. Her voice rose an octave. "So . . ." She cleared her throat. "So, are you moving? I just saw the for-sale sign!"

"It just went up yesterday," he said with a smile. "Donna and I are ready for something new."

Yesterday? Did he just spontaneously decide to move after he murdered Yvette? "You've got the most beautiful house in town! I can't imagine that you've found something better!"

He grinned. "We're moving to Florida! I'm actually heading down today to finalize the details on a set of condos that I have my eye on. I have a little competition, but hopefully I'll be signing the paperwork tomorrow."

Wasn't that convenient? Yvette had stood in his way, and now that she was dead, there was nothing stopping him. Despite his public love for this town, these condos were probably a big deal for him. It meant real money, and if that wasn't a motive, she didn't know what was. She needed to choose her next words carefully. "You're leaving? I had no idea."

"Really?" He frowned. "Janelle knew. That's why I'm selling all of my property. Which reminds me, I haven't heard an update from her. Have you finalized the details with the bank yet?"

"Not yet. Just so busy," Olivia said quickly. "Are you selling your food trucks as well? That's such a shame. I bet Yvette would have loved to own that food truck."

"She actually didn't want to buy," Franklin said with a grimace. "I thought the same thing, but I ended up selling the contract to Jacob."

"Jacob!" Startled, Olivia blinked. "I had no idea that he was interested in the food truck business."

Franklin guffawed. "He's interested in money, my dear. Yvette's food tuck, and the other two that I own, are very lucrative." His tone turned brisk. "Anyway, it was very nice to see you, Olivia. I'm going to be late if I don't run."

"You're flying to Florida now?" she asked in alarm.

He gave her a strange look. "I'm going to the office now. My flight is at nine tonight."

"Of course," she said hastily as she pulled Goodwin out of the way. "I'll see you when you get back."

As she watched him hurry off, her heart sank. Things were working out rather conveniently for him now that Yvette was dead, and it was clear that Nick wasn't treating him as a suspect if he was letting the man jet off to Florida in the middle of the investigation.

If Franklin was guilty, he could be running.

CHAPTER NINE

Rose heard the front door open, and she panicked. What was someone doing in the office at this time of night? Switching off the lamp, she hurried to the closet and closed the doors. A minute later, the door opened and a silhouette appeared in the doorway.

"I don't care who her friends are," a low voice growled. "She's getting too close to the truth, and I want her eliminated!"

Rose felt her heart skip a beat. Someone knew that she was close to the truth, which meant that someone was watching her. She hadn't told anyone.

Except David. Was he betraying her?

The man in the office rifled through the desk before he pulled out a folder and stuffed it in his jacket pocket. Rose narrowed her eyes. She'd bet anything that it was the document she was here for.

Great. Another roadblock. Now what would she do?

When the shower didn't help her clear her mind, Olivia tried to lose herself in the mystery, but she couldn't get Franklin out of her head. What if he was lying? Ripping out her ear buds in frustration, she grabbed her keys and headed to the police station. The only person who could stop Franklin was Nick, and she needed to make sure that he understood the gravity of the situation.

"Olivia!" Deputy Derek Jameson greeted her with a big smile. "I haven't seen you in ages." He swept a hand through his thick hair and gave her an obvious once-over. It was all she could do not to point out how ridiculous he was being. They'd gone to high school together, and he never even gave her the time of day, but when she'd started dating the most-wanted man in town, suddenly Derek decided she was worth pursuing.

"I've seen you," she said and leaned on the front desk. "I even said hi to you last week at End Game, but you were upset about a bet that you'd just lost and were a little too deep in your cups."

Derek winced. "Yeah, I remember that bet, but I don't remember much of the night. I'm sorry I missed you. I don't suppose you're ready to leave that boyfriend of yours and marry me?"

"That boyfriend of mine made me a breakfast sandwich this morning and knew that I might sleep in, so he called me to make sure that I would wake up in time. He's kind of perfect," she admitted with a smile.

Derek grinned. "If you were my girl, I'd make you a three-course meal for breakfast and let you sleep in *all* day. Come on— he's not even local. I remember when you bleached your hair in high school, and it was orange for a week. That alone should earn me a date!"

She cringed. "And that is why I prefer my perfect, non-local boyfriend. Besides, if you were really in love with me, you wouldn't bring that story up. Ever. Is Nick in?"

"Yeah, I think he just got back from lunch. Want me to let him know that you're here?"

And give Nick a chance to duck her? Not a chance. "No. I'll just head back there. I just need to return the key to his house. It'll only take a second." Giving Derek a quick wink, she strolled down the hall to Nick's office and knocked on the door.

"Olivia, is something wrong with Tucker?" he asked on opening the door. Just as she'd expected, he didn't look very pleased. He made the mistake of stepping back, and she slipped into the office. It was sparsely decorated with a fake tree in the corner and several pictures on the desk. Nick and Mary had never had kids, but they both had nieces and nephews they were simply crazy about. The window overlooked the parking lot—Olivia was surprised that Nick hadn't run as soon as he'd seen her green Wrangler pull up.

"No, it's fine. You didn't leave instructions about the key." She gave him a bright smile as she held the key up and then waved it in front of him.

Nick gave her a pointed look. "You've been walking my dog for a year, Olivia. You know where to put the key."

"True, and I really meant to say something to you earlier, but

107

since I'm thinking of putting down roots, I realized that I need contracts. Without contracts, I shouldn't assume that you want me to put the key in your ceramic frog key holder in the back yard. For all I know, you're being extra-vigilant since this horrible crime has been committed. So I'm here officially to ask about the key."

"Did you come with a contract?" he asked with a raised eyebrow.

Crap. "No," she admitted.

"So every time that you walk my dog, I'm supposed to give you instructions about the key? Olivia, you're a horrible liar. What do you want?"

She took a deep breath and tried to steady her nerves. "Franklin Kennedy is leaving town. Tonight."

A shadow passed over his face. "Olivia, I told you to leave this alone. A lot of people didn't get along with Yvette, and I'm not about to accuse the wealthiest, most influential and well-loved man in town of murdering Yvette Dunn. Now, unless you came here with proof, Franklin will go to Florida tonight, and he'll return in three days."

In three days? So Nick did know! Her shoulders slumped. "No, I don't have proof."

"Then you can return my key to the frog. Thank you, Olivia."

"Nick," she whispered. "What is going on with you?"

He leaned against the wall. "I had to do a press release, Olivia. I'm using the facilities at the state police to process a crime. I'm fielding phone calls from the press about updates. There was a murder in our town, Olivia. A murder. That's what's going on with me."

"Right. Of course. I'm sorry, Nick. I really am." Ashamed for thinking that Nick was letting Franklin slide because of their friendship, she placed the key on his desk.

And saw Yvette's open file on his desk.

Don't look, Olivia. Just walk away. Be the good girlfriend. Ignore it.

"Okay, well, I'm going to go. Sorry for bothering you, Nick," she said, and bolted from the office.

"Olivia!" Derek called out as she hurried by. "We could have drinks tonight."

"Busy, gotta go," she said as she raised her hand absently. Derek Jameson was the farthest thing from her mind as she fumbled with her keys and slid into her vehicle.

Maybe that was because Andrew made her a better woman.

And now, she needed his help.

His plans for tonight were about to change, and he was not going to be happy about it.

*   *   *

Knowing that Janelle had the night off so she and Patrick could have date night, Olivia waited for Andrew at Happy Endings. Sneaking a quick look into the kitchen to make sure that Janelle's manager wasn't looking, she snagged a cookie and hurried back to her table.

There were two different places where the residents of Lexingburg dealt with bad days at work. They went to End Game for a drink or they came to Happy Endings for a sugar high. Based on the line that ran out the open door, today had not been a great day for most of the residents.

"Too bad you can't get wine *and* sugar here," Olivia mused. Maybe she'd recommend that Janelle look into expanding.

"Olivia!"

"Crap," she whispered and hastily shoved the rest of the cookie in her mouth. What was her sister doing here? Olivia could really only deal with one issue in her life at a time.

Janelle flashed her a brilliant, peppy smile as she hurried over to the table. "Were we supposed to meet here tonight?"

"No," Olivia muttered through the mouthful of cookie. She swallowed. "No, we weren't. What are you doing here? You're supposed to have dinner with Patrick."

"And I will be, in an hour. I just need to check on the ingredients for tomorrow's delivery orders. Are you stealing my cookies?"

Looking around guiltily, Olivia shrugged. "You were out of scones. You really need to make more scones. Can't you keep some in stock just for me? I'm family."

Janelle rolled her eyes. "Stay away from my cookies *and* my scones, and while you're here, you can sign the paperwork for the bank loan. I've managed to push our meeting until next Monday."

"I meant to tell you that I took the paperwork home, and Goodwin drooled all over it," Olivia lied. "And chewed on it. Sorry."

Her sister didn't look worried. "How many times have I told you that you need to take that dog to obedience classes? It's fine. I made several copies of all the paperwork. Let me check those ingredients, and I'll grab you another folder."

"You made copies? That's so efficient of you," Olivia choked out. "I'm going to need another cookie."

"What was that?"

"Nothing. You look gorgeous! I love that necklace."

111

Janelle's hand went to the strands of rose gold around her neck. "Patrick bought this for me last month! His tastes are evolving. I swear, not six months ago he would have bought me some huge, gaudy hoop earrings. When is Andrew taking you back out?"

Confused by the abrupt change in subject, Olivia blinked. "What?"

"I know that your dinner the other night at L'Amore didn't work out. When is he taking you out again?"

"Wait a minute, he talked to you about my dinner?" Olivia leaned back and crossed her arms. "You seem to talk quite a bit."

"Olivia, don't be so suspicious. Berkeley was the hostess that night. She told me that you showed up in yoga pants. *Yoga* pants, Olivia. It's like you go out of your way to embarrass me. Why didn't you take the green dress?"

It was so hard to keep secrets in a small town. "Things just didn't work out well for me that night. When I was on the way to get the dress, I realized how late I was, so I just skipped a step. He wasn't mad, and Berkeley should learn to keep her mouth shut. She was practically spilling out of her dress and has no room to be talking about *my* inappropriate outfit!"

"So you admit that it was inappropriate?" she smirked.

"Why exactly do you care again?"

Janelle ignored the question. "You are dating a saint. I'm going to get the paperwork. You need to make this up to him, Olivia. He set up a wonderful night for you, and you ruined it."

Guilt washed over her as Janelle left. Her sister didn't know the worst of it. She'd practically spilled beer on the man trying to avoid him and had slept on the couch last night. She really did need to make it up to Andrew in the worst kind of way. Of course, after she asked for the favor she needed from him tonight, he might possibly break up with her.

Leaving her table, she walked around the line and snagged a couple more cookies. The girl at the counter shot her an amused look, and Olivia bought her silence by boxing up a few orders for the guests in line.

"Olivia! My God, are you okay!"

Whirling around, she saw Andrew pushing through the crowd with a frantic look on his face.

"Yeah, I'm fine. Are you okay?"

He stared at her. "Of course I'm not okay. You texted me SOS! I thought you were in an accident. I thought you were hurt!"

"Oh, Andrew," she whispered. She was clearly approaching this all wrong. Hurrying around the counter, she pulled him away from the line and into the corner. "I'm so sorry. I didn't realize that you'd think it was an emergency. I mean, it *is* an emergency, but I'm not hurt."

"SOS means emergency. What the hell is going on, Olivia?"

Wanting to get him out of the bakery before Janelle returned with the paperwork, she pushed him out onto the sidewalk. "I need your help. Your computer skills."

Outside, he turned around and gaped at her. "You texted me SOS because your computer isn't working? Olivia, I think I just lost ten years of my life!"

"And I'm so sorry about that. I promise that I'll make it up to you, but we don't have a lot of time. My computer is fine, but I need some information. Franklin Kennedy is leaving for Florida tonight, and I'm afraid that he killed Yvette and is going to get away with it. I spoke to him . . ."

"You spoke to Franklin Kennedy? Damn it, Olivia, you promised me that you would stay away from this case! This isn't something that you play with! Someone murdered Yvette! Do you understand that?" He grabbed her by the shoulders and shook her.

"I do understand that, but Nick is stretched so thin, Andrew, and Yvette doesn't have anyone to rally for her. She doesn't have any friends or family in the area."

"Sweetheart, the last person who loved Yvette was left standing

114

at the altar—alone."

"And we still don't know why," Olivia said as she searched his face. "Yvette was a private person. We have no idea what was going on in her head, but she was still a member of this town. Someone in this town killed her, and I don't want her murderer to go free. Are you mad at me?" It would be a refreshing change, but she kept that thought to herself, her eyes earnestly locked with his.

His features softened, and he leaned over and kissed her on the forehead. "You're going to make it up to me?"

She should have been relieved, but she only felt coldness spread through her. How could Andrew be so complacent? Taking a deep breath, she plastered a fake smile on her face. She couldn't let her relationship issues get in the way of finding a killer. "A picnic in the park. With cupcakes. Janelle's cupcakes, because you know that I'm a horrible baker."

"Throw in a bottle of wine, and you have yourself a deal." He grinned.

A picnic in the park with wine? It was perfect. Romantic and perfect, but she wasn't about to back out of it now. "Sure," she said softly. "A bottle of wine."

He hooked his arm around her waist and walked with her. "So tell me what you need."

"We know that Yvette was suing him, and it was keeping him from buying the condos in Florida. He told me that he sold the business to Jacob, but I think that he sold the business after Yvette's death. I think he was going to sell it before, and Yvette sued him for breach of contract. If she thought that he was pushing her out of his business, she would have fought like hell, and if he was in breach of their contract, she would have won the lawsuit. I need to know the details and when he sold the company."

"Okay," he said as he hugged her tight. "That's not going to be easy without their social security numbers."

"Well . . ." Olivia deliberately avoided his gaze.

Andrew stopped and stared at her. "You have Yvette's social security number. Why does that not surprise me?"

"I didn't do it on purpose. I just went to the sheriff's station to talk to Nick, and I may have seen some paperwork on the desk and committed Yvette's social security number to memory."

"You are a terrifying woman," he muttered, but she could see the hint of a smile on his face.

She felt a little more in control of the situation as they walked home. Andrew would help her.

Opening a couple of beers, she handed one to Andrew and paced while he hunched over her computer. Too nervous to drink it, she instead tapped her nails nervously against the glass while she waited. Occasionally he looked up and watched her, but she couldn't stop. The very idea that Franklin Kennedy was a killer turned her stomach.

Half an hour later, Andrew looked up from the computer and leaned back in his chair. "I'm sorry, babe, but I don't think Franklin Kennedy is a killer."

Immediately, her hope deflated. "What do you mean? Why?"

"Yvette dropped the lawsuit. She was suing Franklin because he wanted to sell the food truck business in the middle of her rental contract, but when he sold it to Jacob, Jacob re-signed a new contract with Yvette. A three-year contract, which I'm sure made Yvette very happy."

Olivia slumped against the wall. "I was so sure that it was Franklin."

Lifting an eyebrow, Andrew shook his head. "Really? Franklin loves this town. And even though the lawsuit was holding up his new project, it wouldn't have broken him."

"Franklin is fleeing the town that he loves," she pointed out.

"Franklin probably bought those tickets weeks ago, Olivia. Whoever murdered Yvette didn't plan to kill her. They didn't bring a gun or a knife. Whatever happened was spur of the moment."

A crime of passion. That made so much sense. Even Andrew was better at solving crimes than she was. Sighing, Olivia walked over and sank down on Andrew's lap. He immediately put his arm around her and nuzzled her neck. "Are you trying to make me feel better?" she whispered.

"There may be a killer running around this town, and I know you want to be a champion for Yvette, but I have a problem with you throwing yourself into this case."

"But . . ." she protested.

"If you have something that might help Nick investigate, then by all means, help him. But he's the law, Olivia. He's trained to handle situations like this, and you're not. What if Franklin *was* the killer? What do you think would have happened when you questioned him alone today?"

"You're worried," she murmured. "I thought you were trying to tell me that there was nothing to worry about."

"Do I think there's going to be a second killing? No, but that doesn't mean that the killer won't do whatever is necessary to protect themselves. Olivia, I can't lose you."

"You're not going to."

He was silent for a moment as he rested his chin on her head and slowly slid his fingers up and down her arms. Finally, he

118

sighed. "Is there something that you want to tell me, sweetheart?"

Startled, she turned and gazed at him. "What do you mean?"

Reaching out, he swept a strand of hair out of her face and tucked it behind her ear. "I can tell that there's something on your mind, Olivia. Something that's been bothering you all week."

"It's just this thing with Yvette and this thing with Janelle."

"Are you having second thoughts about buying the brownstone? I thought you wanted an office."

Burying her face in his neck, she swallowed hard and lied. "I'm not having second thoughts about anything, Andrew. Everything is just fine."

"I know you, Olivia, and I know that everything is not fine. If you're not ready to tell me, I understand, but you can't lie to me, and more importantly, you can't keep lying to yourself."

Close to tears, she didn't move as she struggled to get her emotions under control. She could count on one hand the number of times Andrew had seen her cry, and it was usually because of her anger rather than sadness or frustration. This was a problem that she couldn't share with him.

He was right about one thing, though.

Everything wasn't fine.

CHAPTER TEN

Rose glared at the detective. "I'm not impeding your investigation. It says right here that your warrant only covers the inside of the house. I'm just searching the shed."

"That's breaking and entering," he growled.

"I have permission," she gloated sassily. "I don't think that Karen killed that man, and I'm going to prove it."

"I thought you were looking for a necklace."

"Well, now I'm doing both. Karen is my link to the necklace, and someone's trying to make sure that I don't have access to her. So you do your thing, but I'm going to clear her name, and I'm going to find my necklace. You, detective, need to stay out of my way."

The handsome man's face darkened when he spun on his heels and walked away. Rose took a moment to admire the way he fit in those pants. If he weren't such an arrogant dick, she might figure out a way to weasel into his arms for a night or two.

"But James is waiting so patiently for you," Olivia protested. "When are you going to realize that he's worth the effort?"

She'd just dropped off her morning dogs and kicked back on the couch to grab a couple more chapters before lunch. She didn't have to walk any dogs until after two, and then she had her out-of-towners tonight. All in all, it was a light day.

It didn't bother her. Next week she had three dogs that would need medicine, and one dog that needed some water therapy. That always paid extra.

Just before Rose Palmer could get down to searching the shed, Olivia's phone rang. With a sigh, she checked it and saw that Andrew was calling. He'd done his best to take her mind off Yvette last night, and it'd worked. She'd actually managed to sleep peacefully in his arms, and she'd been in a fantastic mood this morning. It was time to forget this whole mess with Yvette. She'd given it her best shot, and it just hadn't worked out well.

"Hello, lover boy," she answered with a gleeful smile.

Andrew groaned. "Is Delilah there?" he asked with some trepidation in his voice.

"No, I'm just teasing you. How's your morning going?"

"Busy, but I've been trying to get some things done so I can take a long lunch. Your schedule is clear until mid-afternoon, right?"

"It sure is!"

"Well, it's gorgeous out, and you owe me a picnic."

"Now? I just promised that to you yesterday."

"And I am here to collect. You aren't going to welch on our deal, are you? I happen to remember that you were more than satisfied last night."

Her toes curled at the memory. Despite everything happening, she could always count on the chemistry she had with Andrew. "Are you alluding to your computer skills or that other thing we did last night?"

"My computer skills, of course," he said, widening his eyes with a gasp. "What else would I be talking about?"

Chuckling, she stretched and sat up. "All right. A lunch picnic in the park? I think I could swing that. What kind of sandwiches do you want?"

"I've already got everything taken care of. Meet me in an hour? And leave Goodwin at home."

"Goodwin loves picnics!" Olivia protested. Plus, she might need to use the dog as a distraction if things started to feel a little too romantic.

"Well, I'd like to be able to actually eat my lunch without worrying about whether or not he's going to steal it," Andrew pointed out.

He had a point. Goodwin wasn't a beggar. He was a master thief. He looked for vulnerability, and he used that to his advantage. Take your eye off a sandwich for a single moment, and it was gone.

"His feelings are going to be hurt, but I'll try to make him understand."

"You can always ask about that when you meet with Celeste on Thursday."

Olivia groaned. "How did you hear about that?"

"I have my ways," he said mysteriously. "I've already cleared my schedule because that's something I'm not going to miss."

"Do you want this picnic or not?" she demanded.

"No welching. I'll see you soon, darling." He hung up before she could squeeze more information out of him. Her bets were on Jackie or Janelle spilling the beans, but it was always possible that someone else had told him. Lady Celeste's antics were always a great source of amusement, and the whole town knew about it.

As she headed out the door, she passed Old Man Cramer at his mailbox. He leaned on his cane and scowled at her. "Where are you off to, missy?"

"Good afternoon, Mr. Cramer," she said cheerfully, ignoring his accusing tone. "Are you going to go for a walk? It's a beautiful day!" Despite his age, the older man was actually in great shape and often walked around town. He liked to take notes in his little notebook and report everything that he deemed as a crime to the police. A few times, Olivia had been the perpetrator of those crimes because Cramer was certain that she was using the dogs to break into people's homes. Of course, despite his great physical shape, his mind was deteriorating. When he reported Olivia, he didn't always *know* that he was reporting *Olivia*.

"Someone has to keep an eye on this town. That lovely girl was murdered, and that sheriff is no help! No help at all!"

A week ago, that lovely girl had been a gypsy, no doubt peddling drugs from her truck. Olivia held back a smile. "Sheriff Limperos is spending every waking minute trying to solve her crime. I'm sure that it was just someone passing through. He'll catch them, and we won't have anything to worry about."

"Shiny baubles," he muttered. "Shiny baubles."

Cramer's nonsensical mutterings reminded Olivia of the ring that Andrew was probably carrying around in his pocket—and the romantic picnic she was about to be late for. "Mr. Cramer, is your nurse coming today?"

"Lydia? She's late. She's always late," he muttered as he started back to the house. "She's going to forget my chicken salad, too."

Lydia was never late, and she never forgot the chicken salad. She was the reason that Cramer didn't have to live in a nursing home.

Waving goodbye, Olivia headed to the park. It faced several of the businesses behind Main Street, and while it didn't attract a lot of tourist attention, it was the perfect spot for locals. The mayor wanted to add picnic tables and vending carts to lure in visitors, but the town always vetoed it. Lexingburg liked their secret oasis.

There were only a few people scattered about, so it wasn't hard to spot Andrew. He was still dressed in his business suit and sprawled out on a checkered red and white blanket. He had a large basket, two wine glasses with a bottle of red, sandwiches, chips, and cupcakes. It looked like a scene out of a picture book.

"I didn't think they actually made red-and-white checkered blankets," Olivia commented as she approached him. "I thought they were just in movies and television shows."

"Hey, I hold nothing back for you," he said as he pushed himself up and leaned over to give her a kiss. "I had Janelle make your favorite."

Olivia's stomach rumbled in anticipation. "Turkey with grape jelly?"

"Exactly how did you get onto that combination?" he asked as he poured the wine.

"Janelle made me eat it on a dare when we were kids. Joke's on her because I loved it! It's the most amazing thing ever, and I take personal offense that you won't at least try it."

"For the sake of our relationship, I think it's best if I don't," Andrew said with a grimace. "I've also got jalapeño chips and black-and-white cupcakes."

"Is it my birthday? This is amazing," she said thoughtlessly. An unreadable expression settled on his face, and she hurried to change the subject. "Have you heard any updates about Yvette's case?"

"The case that you're not supposed to be thinking about anymore?" he reminded her gently.

Scowling, she took a bite of her sandwich. "Everyone in town is talking about it. You can't be mad at me for showing interest."

"As long as that interest doesn't lead to any actions on your part." He watched her intently. "Slow down. You don't have to inhale your sandwich."

Slow down? It wasn't like Andrew to criticize her. She went to take another bite before an unwelcome idea occurred to her. Some men put engagement rings in glasses of champagne and decadent desserts. Her boyfriend wouldn't put one in her turkey and jelly sandwich—would he?

Clearing her throat, she slowly put the sandwich down and reached for her wine. Trying not to seem too obvious, she swirled the glass and checked it for foreign objects. Satisfied that there were no rings hidden inside, she took a sip.

Now she wasn't even going to be able to enjoy her sandwich. With a forced smile, she reached for her plate again and focused only on her chips. She would fill up on those and ignore the sandwich. He wouldn't force feed it to her, and that would buy her a little more time.

"These chips are so good," she moaned. "Anyway, you didn't answer my question."

"I haven't heard any updates on Yvette's death, but I've heard rumors. Someone at the hospital suggested that the psychic did it."

"People in Lowell are talking about the murder?" The city dwellers didn't usually concern themselves with small town concerns, despite the fact that they were neighbors.

"The press release was national. *Everyone* is talking about it," Andrew pointed out. "Do you remember our first date?"

"I remember that you think dinner at Hollendale's was our first date, and I still have to remind you that simply because we were both there at the same time, and simply because you chose to sit next to me at the bar and bother me, it does not actually count as a date. Our first date was a month later when you took me to that fancy steak place in Lowell. Stagwaff?"

"Wagstaff, and I told you that I'd be at Hollendale's, so you obviously followed me there so we could have dinner together," he said with a smile. "It does count as a first date."

"I didn't follow you there," she protested in an exasperated voice. "You never told me that you would be at Hollendale's, and if you did, I wasn't paying attention. You just want to believe that was our first date because it went better than our *actual* first date."

He chuckled. "You asked our waiter if you could have ketchup with your steak. I thought he was going to have a stroke right there at the table."

"I didn't want it for the steak! I thought I was getting fries! I had no idea that they didn't serve fries there."

"I knew you were going to be a handful," he muttered as he took a sip of his wine. "And I was right. How's your sandwich?"

"Should you be drinking? Aren't you going back to work?"

"I don't think a glass is going to hurt. I'm an IT guy, not a doctor."

"You're not just any IT guy. You're *the* IT guy."

"You're not eating your sandwich."

"Is that Kristy? That's totally Kristy!" Giddy with relief, she watched Janelle's real estate agent walk out of one of the offices across the street. This was her only chance to escape the perfect proposal moment. "I'm so sorry, Andrew, but I still have some questions for her."

"You could call her," he pointed out. "She'd be more than happy to take your call, considering that you've been ducking hers."

"Not ducking," Olivia said as she scrambled to her feet. "Just busy. I'll only be a few minutes."

"Olivia, I only have a few minutes!"

She was already off the blanket and hating herself. "I'll be right back," she called over her shoulder as she hurried to intercept Kristy.

The perky brunette was dressed in a sharp khaki skirt and a bright pink button-up shirt. She always had a large smile on her face and a bubbly personality, but Olivia suspected that was a perquisite for all real estate agents. Part of the reason that Olivia ducked her calls was because the woman's voice had a way of grating on her nerves.

Right then, Olivia didn't care if the woman sounded like Minnie Mouse. Kristy was her salvation. "Kristy! Kristy!"

"Olivia!" Surprise filled the woman's face, but it was immediately replaced by that million-watt smile. "What a lovely surprise! I was just on my way to see your sister, to get an update on your sale. Are you meeting us there?"

Great. That wasn't what she wanted to hear. The last thing that she wanted to do was meet with Kristy and Janelle together. "I," she swallowed hard, "I had a few questions that I wanted to ask you."

"I am more than happy to answer any questions that you have! Walk with me!"

"Actually, I was just going to ask them right here." She glanced nervously over her shoulder to see the annoyed expression on Andrew's face. It was entirely possible that when this was all over, she wouldn't just not have a fiancée. She wouldn't have a boyfriend.

"You aren't going to the meeting?"

"I wasn't planning on it. I'm actually having a picnic with Andrew right now."

"Okay. Well, what were your questions?"

Immediately, Olivia's mind went blank. She did have questions about the sale. She had a world of questions, but at that very minute, she couldn't think of any. "Um ... what could we negotiate on the inspection report? I know there were quite a few pages of repairs that could be made."

Kristy gave her an answer that she already knew. "Franklin Kennedy is looking for a quick sale, so he's not offering to make any of the repairs, but he'll greatly reduce the price to make up for it. We spoke about that last week."

"Yes, I remember that now." She glanced over her shoulder again, and her heart sank when she saw Andrew packing up the picnic.

Kristy caught that too. "It looks like your picnic is over. So I guess you'll be joining Janelle and me for our meeting?"

"Yes," she said dejectedly. "It looks like I am. You go ahead. I'm going to tell Andrew goodbye."

Kristy waved cheerfully at Andrew and nodded her head before heading to Happy Endings. With her heart in her stomach, Olivia jogged back to Andrew. "You're leaving?"

"I'm on my lunch break, Olivia. I didn't have a lot of time,"

"Are you mad? I'm so sorry. I just saw Kristy and . . ." words failed her. How could she explain her actions without admitting that she was ducking his proposal?

"I'm not mad," he said as he leaned over and kissed her forehead. "I should have planned it when we had more time. I just got so excited when I saw how nice the weather was today."

Incredulous, she searched his face. "You're not mad at me? Are you sure? I think I'd be furious."

"You have a lot going on. I get that."

Her shoulders dropping, she stepped back. "Okay, well, Kristy is on her way to talk to Janelle, so I guess I should go be there for that."

"That's a good thing. She can answer all your questions, and you can get the ball rolling. That's what you want, right?"

How many times was he going to ask her that question? Not wanting to lie to him anymore, she gave him a small smile. "Thanks for thinking of me today. I'll make it up to you."

"You're racking things up, Olivia. Don't think I'm not keeping track."

Sure, he was keeping track of the times that she'd abandoned him, but he couldn't have the decency to call her out on it. He was so passionate in other aspects of their relationship, but so cold in others. Didn't he care?

An alarming thought ran through her head. Andrew didn't do short-term relationships. He had been with his ex-girlfriend for four years before life got in the way and split them up. What if this wasn't about love? What if this was just his way of making certain that history didn't repeat itself?

Maybe that was why she didn't want to say yes. Maybe, subconsciously, she knew that something was wrong. Maybe Andrew didn't want to marry her so much as he just wanted to finally be married.

132

CHAPTER ELEVEN

In an attempt to push that horrible feeling away, Olivia shoved her ear buds into her ears to listen to more Rose Palmer as she slowly walked to Happy Endings, but her heart wasn't in it. The low and sexy voice of the narrator discussed the obvious spark between Rose and the detective, but she was rooting for James, the patient and understanding lover who was waiting for Rose to realize that they were meant to be together.

Maybe Rose kept him at a distance because she understood that they simply didn't fit. Maybe James was yearning for something that was never going to be.

Olivia used to constantly walk away from Andrew. Even now, she was pushing him away, but he never let her go. She'd thought that it was romantic, but maybe Andrew was just making sure that he was getting a solid return on his investment.

By the time she made it to the bakery, she was disgusted with Rose Palmer. Maybe everyone was right. It was time for her to get her head out of her mystery books and focus on reality. If she'd done it sooner, she would have seen this coming.

"Olivia!" Janelle opened the door excitedly. "I put a lot of effort into that picnic, but I'm too happy to be mad. I didn't think I'd get you and Kristy in the same room ever again. She tells me that you have questions? Why didn't you tell me that you have questions?"

"You don't always listen," Olivia said under her breath.

"What was that?" Janelle ran her hands through her short hair, and flour dust rose in the air.

"Nothing! If I'm going to do this, I'm going to need coffee and a vanilla scone. Actually, make that a cannoli. Please tell me that you have cannolis."

Janelle smiled and pointed to the table. "I have two waiting for you."

"Wow. That's actually really sweet of you. Thanks."

"Olivia, I've known you your whole life. Don't act so surprised. Now come on!"

The lunch crowd had already left, and the small cafe was empty, so there would be no distractions for her. Sitting in front of Kristy and that terrifyingly happy smile was one of the scariest things she'd ever done. If the coffee wasn't so piping hot, she would have guzzled it to fortify herself.

"Is Andrew as excited as you are about the sale?" Kristy asked.

"More," Olivia said honestly. "He's just thrilled about it!"

"Well, I know that you have some questions, but I want to point out that buying the brownstone before it hits the market is your best chance at snatching it up at rock-bottom pricing. Mr. Kennedy would like the sale to go through as quickly as possible, but once other people start showing interest, he may relax a little and decide to wait for the highest bidder."

"I'm sold," Janelle said instantly. "I'd like Franklin to replace the pipes, but at this price, I'm sure that we could afford to fix it, right?"

Olivia gave her an incredulous look. "Janelle, you've used most of your credit to get the bakery started. Even with the low mortgage rate and amazing price, you don't have the kind of savings that would cover any big repairs, and replacing the pipes is a huge repair."

"I've done an estimate on the pipe and roofing repair. Based on your finances, we'll easily be able to make the down payment and still have enough left over to make the required updates," Janelle said cheerfully.

Gaping at her older sister, Olivia tried not to lose her temper. "Based on my finances? How did you get my finances?"

Kristy's smile slipped just a little. "We went over all the finances the last time we got together. You weren't at that meeting."

"That's right, and I couldn't get a hold of you, so I spoke to Andrew . . ."

Olivia held up her hand to stop her sister. "You talked to Andrew about my finances? You talked to him about this sale? Why?"

Her sister cocked her head in confusion. "I don't see why you're so upset. I talked to Patrick as well."

"Of course you talked to Patrick. You're married! Your finances are all tied together, and he's got a stake in this business!"

Janelle sighed. "Is that what this is about? Sweetie, you have nothing to worry about. You and Andrew will be married soon enough, so of course he cares about your future."

"Really?" Olivia felt her control slip. "We're going to be married soon enough? I don't believe that I've discussed marriage to Andrew with anyone, and it certainly shouldn't be a discussion in my financial business."

Janelle obviously didn't understand the root of Olivia's anger. "Andrew knows how you feel about him. You two don't need to discuss marriage. It's a given. Are you concerned that you're going into this alone? You're not! Andrew has your back, and so do I!"

Clenching her teeth, Olivia was about to tell Janelle that she didn't need her support when the bell over the door rang. Taking a deep, steadying breath, she watched Janelle get up to handle the new customer.

It was Samantha. Kristy's eyes widened in surprise, and she ducked her head. "Do you know who that is?" she whispered.

"I do," Olivia said slowly.

The real estate agent put a hand over her heart. "My goodness, that's right! You found poor Yvette's body! What was that like?"

Shifting uncomfortably in her seat, Olivia wondered how she could have such rotten luck. First she'd used Kristy to avoid Andrew, only to find herself in another situation that she didn't want to be in. Now she had a chance to avoid this situation, but it meant gossiping about the murder that she wasn't supposed to be talking about. What was going to happen next? Was her mother going to walk in? . . . because that would just be the icing on the cake!

"It was startling," Olivia muttered.

"Startling? I think I would have screamed my little head off."

"Well, Andrew was there."

"Oh, I bet he held your hand the whole time and just took complete charge of the situation, didn't he?"

Was this woman from the 1950s? "No. I held my own," Olivia said frostily.

"How's the investigation going? I heard that you and Andrew

exonerated Janelle. Does that mean that there's another suspect?"

"I don't know any more than what the news is reporting."

Kristy's face fell in disappointment. "I think that it was a lovers' quarrel. The thought helps me sleep better at night."

"Lovers' quarrel?" Despite her promise to Andrew—and to herself, Olivia's interest was piqued. "Was Yvette dating someone?"

"Well, Jacob, of course!"

Olivia moved her head to see Samantha's petite frame standing at the counter. "Jacob? He and Yvette broke up! I thought he was with Samantha," she said in a hushed voice.

"They did break up, but when Jacob took over the food truck business, I heard that they rekindled their romance. He and Samantha never got back together. They just hang out as friends."

"I don't understand. Yvette left him at the altar. Why would he give her another chance?"

Kristy shrugged. "I don't know the particulars, but I heard them fighting in the food truck one night. He was accusing her of being afraid of commitment. Afraid to marry him and afraid to go into business with him."

It was a crime of passion. Even Andrew knew enough to see

that, and it looked like no one was more passionate about Yvette than Jacob. A secret rekindled affair? History repeating itself? Had Jacob decided that enough was enough?

"But I've seen him with Samantha. They were at L'Amore the other night. Why would he take her to a fancy restaurant if they weren't dating?"

Kristy shrugged. "I don't know. I would assume that with their history, he turned to Samantha when things went sour the first time with Yvette. I guess he just needed a friend."

Before she could ask for more details, the bell on the door sounded again. "Darlings!" a familiar voice rang out. "I had no idea that I'd find you both here."

Olivia groaned. She just had to put it out there in the universe. As if to prove that the universe really could make things worse, it sent her mother.

CHAPTER TWELVE

"Mom!" Olivia rose from her seat and forced a smile while her mother embraced her. It wasn't hard to see who Olivia and Janelle got their looks from. Pamela Rickard had the same dark, thick hair and great legs, but her complexion was soft and creamy, and her eyes were hazel. Though she was pushing sixty, she was in great shape and always seemed to crackle with energy

While Janelle and their mother got along great, Olivia had a strained relationship with both of her parents. Her mother didn't approve of her flighty lifestyle and wanted her to make some permanent life choices. Pamela was over the moon with Andrew and was even warming up to Olivia's dog-walking business. It felt almost strange for Olivia to see her mother so happy with her.

"I can't believe everything that I've missed while I'm gone! It's just horrible what happened to Yvette, and Olivia, darling, why did you have to go get mixed up in it?"

"Mixed up in it?" Olivia pulled back and frowned. "I just found her. Janelle was a suspect!"

"Gee, thanks," Janelle said dryly as she opened the door for Samantha to leave.

Pamela rolled her eyes. "I'm sure she wasn't a suspect. Nick is a smarter man than that. Why do you have to exaggerate everything, Olivia?"

"I don't know, am I exaggerating things, Janelle?" Olivia asked pointedly as she eyed her sister.

Her mother interrupted before Janelle could say anything. "Olivia, I know you. You don't get involved with things like this unless you're afraid of something. You're just distracting yourself."

"What on earth could I possibly be afraid of?" Olivia protested.

Pamela continued as though her daughter hadn't spoken. "Janelle, do you remember when Olivia was fourteen and about to go to summer camp? It was a three-week experience at Lake Hurst, and Olivia was so upset when she realized that you weren't going with her that she started pulling the criminal reports from the area. A week before camp, she had us all convinced that there was a serial killer in the area!"

"Excuse me?" Olivia said as she crossed her arms. "To this day, you still can't prove that there wasn't a serial killer in the area. It's like you don't even care about my safety."

"I do care about your safety, darling, which is why I'm concerned about you and this murder."

Kristy sensed the tension and immediately jumped in. "Ladies, I am so sorry, but I have another meeting to get to, and I just realized that I left the paperwork back at the office. I can see that you two still have a few things to discuss, so why don't we reschedule this for Friday?"

"That would be great," Olivia gushed. "We certainly wouldn't want to make you late for your next appointment."

"But Olivia, we still need to get the ball rolling," Janelle protested.

"As you already pointed out, we have to sign the papers and submit them to the bank before we can do anything else," Olivia said quickly. "I promise that next time we meet, we'll know for sure if we're going to get the brownstone."

"What do you mean, if?" Pamela asked with a frown. "Is there some reason that you might not get it?"

"I'm sure Olivia just means that we'll know for sure if the bank will approve the loan," Janelle interjected. "Mom, you want some coffee?"

"Yes, I would. We came straight from the airport. Joseph went back to the house to check on Nikita. Olivia, I really think you need to expand your business to include cats!"

"I told you that I could stop by the house and check on her, but I couldn't take her. Goodwin doesn't get along with cats." It was like arguing with a brick wall.

Janelle smirked as she brought over a mug and poured their coffee. "Maybe you can ask Celeste about that on Thursday."

Pamela's eyes widened in horror, and she pressed her hand to her lips. "Olivia, you're not indulging Lady Celeste's delusions, are you?"

"I didn't mean to," Olivia grumbled. "Weren't we talking about Yvette's murder?"

"I saw the news while we were on vacation, and I called Nick right away. Olivia, he said that you and Andrew found the body. Was it just horrible? Oh, my poor baby!"

"She means Andrew," Janelle joked.

"Stop that. Of course I mean Olivia. Sweetheart, are you okay?"

Olivia sighed and started to look for a quick exit. What she wouldn't give for another interruption by an arriving customer. First her mother accused her of deliberately getting involved, and now she was *poor baby*. "Mom, I'm fine. Andrew's fine. We were just shocked, that's all."

"Well, Nick wanted me to let you know that you need to quit meddling. Olivia, you aren't trying to get more involved, are you? You could make things worse if you don't let Nick do his job."

It was like listening to a broken record. "Mom, I only got involved because Janelle was a suspect. I told Andrew that I was going to let it go, and I have. For the most part," she added quickly.

"And how are things with you and Andrew?"

Olivia narrowed her eyes. There was a strange tone in her mom's voice, and she was staring at Olivia's fingers. Andrew was a traditional man. It wouldn't surprise her if he'd asked her parents for their blessing before proposing to her. It was one thing for her sister to know, but her mom, too? Pamela was probably over the moon, thinking that she would finally get to see her youngest daughter married.

Still, Olivia had the advantage. The proposal was probably supposed to be a surprise, so her mom couldn't actually talk with her about it. "We're fine, why?" she asked innocently. "Is there a reason that we wouldn't be fine?"

"What . . .? —no!" Pamela said quickly. "I just . . . with the murder . . . you hadn't mentioned him, that's all."

Olivia hid a smile. "I just mentioned him," she pointed out. "And you've been here all of ten minutes."

"Right," her mom said hastily. "You should bring him over. Joseph and I will cook. Janelle, you and Patrick can join us. It'll be a family dinner! Oh, we haven't done one of those in such a long time!"

"I'll have to check my schedule," Olivia said vaguely.

"Yes, we do have a lot on our plate."

Shooting her sister a strange look, Olivia saw Janelle looking meaningfully at their mother. Janelle didn't come to her aid often, so something else was going on here.

Awkward silence descended on Happy Endings as her sister and her mother both stared at her. "What? Do I have something on my face?"

"Don't you have some dogs to take out?" Janelle asked pointedly.

"Sure, in an hour."

Pamela smiled. "Oh, you can spend the next hour with us? How wonderful!"

"No." Olivia shook her head and immediately stood. "No, I cannot, because I have to look over all these files that Janelle keeps giving me. Bye, Mom. We'll talk later."

Leaning over, she gave her mom a peck on the cheek and ignored Janelle's silent gloating. They were going to talk about her as soon as she left, but at least Janelle had given her an out.

Heading next door to Shelfie, she found Jackie on a stepladder, dusting the top shelf of the non-fiction section. "Did you know that Jacob and Yvette were back together?"

Jackie paused and looked over her shoulder. "Are you really here talking about the case, or are you avoiding your mom?"

"How did you know that my mom was here?"

"She stopped by with a gift." Reaching over, Jackie snagged a snow globe and tossed it down. Olivia caught it easily and smiled when she shook it. It was a vineyard surrounding a large wine bottle, with glitter falling all around it.

"She didn't buy *me* a gift," Olivia muttered as she handed the gift back.

"Oh, stop. It's for my collection, and I paid her for it. To answer your original question, I did hear a rumor that Yvette and Jacob were spending more time together, but I never saw them together. Why do you ask?"

"Samantha came into the bakery while Kristy and I were talking. Samantha and Jacob are always together, so I assumed that they were a couple again. I saw them in L'Amore the other night!"

Jackie snorted as she climbed down and adjusted the glasses on her face. "What were you doing in L'Amore?"

"Andrew took me there," Olivia admitted. "I think he's going to propose."

Eyes widening, Jackie snapped her head up. "Really? What makes you say that?"

"Just a feeling that I get."

"Are you going to say yes?" Jackie headed to the back of the bookstore and pointed to a box. Olivia bent down to pick one up and followed Jackie back to the shelf that she was cleaning. The bookstore owner started re-shelving the new books.

"I don't know. I keep making up excuses and finding distractions whenever it looks like he's going to propose. I almost spilled a beer on him at End Game in an effort to get him to stop talking!"

"Have you lost your mind? Half this town wants to marry Andrew, and he's in love with you. You're in love with him. What's the problem?"

Tugging on her ponytail, Olivia shrugged and winced. "I do love him, but I'm not sure that he's proposing for the right reasons. I feel like he thinks that it's the next natural step in the relationship, and that's not why two people should get together."

"And your reason for that insane line of thinking?"

"I showed up at L'Amore dressed in yoga pants and a tank top. I ignored his request to keep my nose out of Yvette's case. Just today I ruined the picnic that he'd planned, and not once has he gotten angry with me!"

"Poor Olivia," Jackie mocked. "She has the perfect and most

patient boyfriend. I can see why that would make you not want to marry him. He's terrible."

"I know it sounds ridiculous, but it's this fear that I can't shake. Something is wrong."

"The only thing wrong here is your fear of commitment. You're like the guy in the relationship," Jackie said as she reached down for another book. "You're creating problems where there aren't any to cover up your guilt for not wanting to marry the perfect man."

"I'm sorry, I thought you owned a bookstore. I had no idea that you're a psychologist," Olivia said, feeling surly. "I have no problems with commitment. I commit all the time. Just a few minutes ago, I committed to the idea of avoiding all family dinners with my mother and sister. That's a lifetime of dodging invitations. It's a *huge* commitment!"

"Haha. Face it, Olivia, you have a problem. You don't like change. You could have signed for the brownstone by now, but you haven't."

"That has nothing to do with commitment and everything to do with Janelle acting like she's doing me a favor!"

"Then *tell* her. Explain the problem, work it out, and get yourself an office. It's an easy fix."

Olivia grumbled. "I hate you. You know that, right? I'm going to find a new best friend."

"Delilah is two doors down. I bet she'd love to be your friend!"

"Shut up." Olivia laughed. "Delilah would drop dead if I offered to be her friend. Actually, that could work in my favor."

"You want my advice? Spend some time with Janelle when you two aren't talking about the brownstone. Just hang out, as sisters, rather than potential partners. And don't doubt how Andrew feels for you. Any moron can see that he's crazy about you."

"Maybe you're right," Olivia murmured. "All right. I've got to pick up Snowball and Tucker. Because I'm a dog walker. I've committed myself to walking dogs. Would someone who fears commitment be doing that?"

"You're impossible," Jackie said loudly as Olivia skipped out of the store. "You're in denial! You could quite possibly be insane."

"Quit reading those self-help books!" Olivia said quickly before she shut the door behind herself.

Afraid of commitment? Olivia had never heard anything so ridiculous. She loved commitment. Reveled in it. She committed to everything, and Jackie had no idea what she was talking about.

149

CHAPTER THIRTEEN

Andrew had returned from his failed picnic with Olivia feeling more frustrated than ever. He'd simply been trying to have a good time with Olivia without the pressure of proposing to her, and even that couldn't go right. His complicated girlfriend hadn't even eaten her favorite sandwich, and she'd looked miserable when she'd said goodbye to him.

He'd give just about anything to figure out what was going on in her mind.

Too bad he couldn't solve his own problems as easily as this one. Leaning back in the chair, he finished rebooting the computer and smiled when it started up perfectly. "All right, Debbie, you're all set. Next time it freezes, try not to resort to violence. Computers don't really respond well to that."

"Thanks, Andrew. I'm sorry. It's just been doing that all week, and my patience finally snapped."

"That's why you call me when you *first* start having problems and not when you're ready to commit murder." Smiling at the insurance counselor, he handed her the final forms that she needed to sign. Happy that another crisis was averted, he took the elevator back up to his office and found the sheriff sitting outside. Poor Cora looked at him, terror in her eyes.

"Nick," he said smoothly as he handed the paperwork to Cora. "Can you go ahead and file this?" he whispered.

"Andrew, why are the police here for you? Should I call security?"

"Sheriff Limperos trumps security," Andrew said with a chuckle. "But thanks for looking out for me."

Opening the door, he waved the sheriff inside. Nick cleared his throat and grimaced. "I don't mean to interrupt you while you're at work, Andrew, but I was hoping to speak to you without Olivia around."

Gesturing for Nick to sit down, Andrew slid his hands nervously over his shirt. "What did she do now? She promised that she'd stay away from the case."

"No, it's nothing like that. I just didn't want her to know that I need your help."

"My help? What's going on?"

"We have Yvette's computer, and it wasn't hard to discover her password, but no one in the department is a whiz at computers, and I'm afraid if I ask the state police for more help, they'll take over the whole investigation."

Understanding dawned on Andrew. "You want me to look it over?"

"If you wouldn't mind. Do you have a second?"

"I don't, but if you want to stop by my apartment tonight, we can look it over then." Andrew saw Nick's hesitation and smiled knowingly. "Don't worry. Olivia and I don't have any plans tonight, and I want to keep her as far away from this as possible. She has a way of finding trouble, and she doesn't seem to realize that she could be putting herself in danger."

"She doesn't give up easily," Nick agreed. "I can be at your place around seven. How does Chinese food sound?"

"Sounds perfect."

"Thanks again, Andrew. I need a break in this case. I feel like the whole town is breathing down my neck."

Andrew pitied the man. There were dark circles under his eyes, as though he hadn't slept for months. "You'll catch them, Nick. I've got faith in you."

Nick just grunted in return before shuffling out the office. Andrew could tell that the case was weighing heavily on his shoulders. Nick wasn't the kind of man who worked well under pressure, and he was probably getting it on all sides. Andrew was more than happy to help.

So long as Olivia didn't find out.

That night, after ducking Olivia's apology phone call and texting her a vague message about hanging out with a friend tonight, he opened a couple of beers with Nick and sat down at the breakfast bar after plugging in and opening Yvette's computer. "All right. Let's see what this bad boy has. Password?"

"Coffee4all79. All lowercase letters. The 'for' is a number," Nick said as he flipped through the pages of his notebook. "The deputies just found her financials on QuickBooks and a bunch of photos. She was making enough money to live off of, but not enough to kill her for. No photos of friends or family. Most of them are of her and Jacob when they were dating."

Nick wasn't wrong. There were no documents or games on the computer, but Yvette had used it to back up her phone. Andrew opened up the photo files and frowned as he flipped through them. "Olivia told me that Jacob and Samantha were dating. We saw them at L'Amore the other night."

The sheriff pulled the boxes of Chinese food from the bag and slid one across the counter. "When I talked to Jacob, he said that he wasn't seeing anyone. He and Yvette were business partners, and he and Samantha were just good friends. According to him, he and Yvette were on good terms. They'd put that whole wedding business behind them."

"That's probably true, because these photos of Yvette with Jacob are recent. Most of these were taken in the city of Lowell.

153

See this deli? It's right across from the hospital. Look at the sign."

Andrew turned the laptop around, and Nick put on his glasses and leaned over the counter. The photo was a selfie of Yvette and Jacob kissing. "It says that hospital employees get thirty percent off six-inch subs. Nice discount."

"It is a nice discount," Andrew agreed. "And it just started three weeks ago."

"Jacob has an alibi for the morning of Yvette's murder. He was with Franklin," Nick said with a sigh. "If I bring him in for questioning, Franklin will throw a fit."

"You're worried about Franklin?"

"No, I'm worried about his girlfriend, the mayor," Nick said with a rueful smile. "He found out that Olivia was asking questions about his intentions, and I got yelled at for an hour for letting a civilian get in the way. Even though he's in Florida, Franklin still protects his good name."

"Photos don't mean anything," Andrew said with a shrug. "They could just be celebrating their new partnership. Did you guys get into her emails?"

"Yeah, but it was business stuff."

Andrew opened his box of sesame chicken and dug in with a plastic fork. Bringing up the browser, he found the bookmark for email. "She probably has a separate account for her personal and business email, but if she used Gmail for both, they're probably linked." Clicking on the small icon in the corner, he smiled when another email dropped down. "Here we go."

After opening Yvette's personal email, he slid the laptop back over to Nick. A few minutes later, Nick frowned. "Most of it is spam. She exchanged a few emails with a friend, but it's nothing to break the case open." He returned the computer to Andrew.

"Not everyone uses email today. Especially with texting," Andrew explained with a shrug. An idea occurred to him, and he opened the command center to the computer. "Most people back their photos up to the cloud, so if something is deleted from the phone, it's not necessarily deleted from the computer. Here we go. Yvette took a bunch of screenshots from her phone a few days before she was killed. They're texts from Jacob, and they're not nice. Did you see anything like that on her phone?"

"No. There was nothing to connect Jacob and Yvette on her phone. She didn't even have his number stored. Let me see?"

"It looks like Jacob wanted more than Yvette was willing to give," Andrew said softly. For a minute, he actually felt bad for the poor guy.

Nick looked over Andrew's shoulder and whistled low between his teeth. "'Not nice' is an understatement. It looks like Jacob thought Yvette was just using him. Why would she take a picture of the texts? Why would she delete them?"

"I don't know, but that sounds like motive to me."

The sheriff sighed and shook his head. "You were supposed to make my life easier, Andrew. Not harder. How's your proposal going?"

In the middle of taking a swig of beer, Andrew choked on it and glared. "How do you know about that?"

"Janelle babbles when she's nervous. When I interrogated her, I learned more than I wanted to know about her husband, and she spoke at length about how she'd orchestrated a romantic evening so you could propose to Olivia. I haven't seen a ring on her finger."

Andrew smiled and reached into his pocket to pull out the ring. Opening the small box, he revealed the round-cut one-and-a-half carat diamond in its platinum setting.

"Wow," Nick whistled. "That is some ring."

"Thanks. I've had it for a while. It's perfect for Olivia. Unfortunately, all of my attempts at proposing have failed. I've trying to wait for the right moment, rather than forcing it."

"I'm pretty sure everyone is taking bets. It's even worse than when Yvette and Jacob were engaged."

Andrew gritted his teeth. Living in a small town had its drawbacks. "Bets? That's just fantastic. This proposal is going to have to be a surgical strike, and half the town is betting against me, I'm sure. I don't know, Nick. I've started to ask her a couple of times, but something isn't right. I thought it was just the sale of the brownstone bothering her, but now I'm afraid it's something more. I know she's a difficult woman, but I was so sure that she'd be ready. What if I've misread everything?"

Nick reached over and clasped him on the shoulder. "The town isn't betting against you, Andrew. Well, I take that back. I'm pretty sure most of the females are hoping she turns you down, but this town loves Olivia. They want to see her happy, and she does love you. Believe me, I've never seen her like this with anyone, ever before."

"Thanks for that. I haven't given up. I figure, instead of trying to plan the perfect moment, I'll just wait for the perfect moment to come to us."

"That's a good idea. I've known Olivia since she was just a little girl. She's cautious by nature."

"Not cautious enough," Andrew said with a sigh. "Let's see what else we can find, shall we? The sooner you close the case, the sooner I can have my girlfriend's attention again."

*   *   *

"Do you think he was hanging out with Brett?" Olivia asked Jackie anxiously. "Brett has the single life down. He's probably trying to convince Andrew not to ask me to marry him."

After Andrew's vague text the night before, that he was hanging out with friends, Olivia hadn't been able to stop obsessing about it. Impending proposal aside, Andrew had been acting strange lately.

"Would you prefer that? Snowball, don't eat that!" Jackie snapped. She tugged at the dog's leash, but the Rottweiler, dressed in a purple tutu, paid no attention to her.

Olivia snapped her fingers and used her hip to push the dog away from the glass bottle on the sidewalk. Picking it up, she tossed it in the nearby trashcan and kept walking. "Brett wants Andrew to be single so he can be the perfect wingman. *That* I definitely don't want. I took your advice and asked Janelle to have dinner with me tonight."

"In public? So you two can have a civil conversation without fighting?"

"We're not going to fight. We're not even going to talk about the sale. I'm going to cook dinner, and we're just going to hang out."

They walked by the condos on Fourth Street, and Jackie threw back her head and laughed. "You told her that you were cooking, and she still agreed to come over?"

"I can cook," Olivia said defensively. "Velveeta cheese shells. I was thinking that maybe you should come over and join us. You know, act as a buffer."

"Fine, I'll come by, but only if I can cook. You just provide the wine."

Everything was working out just the way Olivia had planned. "I can handle that," she said with a devious grin.

"You did that on purpose," Jackie accused.

"Maybe," Olivia murmured, but something else had caught her eye. "Isn't that Samantha over there?" The woman standing on the sidewalk was dressed in cream pants and a gorgeous pink blouse. Her hair curled around her shoulders, and even behind her large sunglasses, it was impossible to miss that signature pout.

"Probably. Jacob lives in one of these condos."

"Samantha!" Olivia called out and quickened her pace. Goodwin gave a bound of glee and then, at a tug of the leash, trotted next to her.

"Olivia!" Jackie hissed. "What are you doing?"

"I told you what Kristy said yesterday," Olivia whispered back. "Samantha!"

Samantha turned around with a tight smile. "Olivia. Jackie.

How are you?"

"Good. Good. Just out walking Goodwin and Snowball."

Samantha frowned. "Is that dog wearing a tutu?"

"Yeah, Snowball likes to show off his feminine side. I saw you in the bakery yesterday, and I feel absolutely terrible about not saying hello to you. We were in the middle of a meeting with Kristy, and then my mom walked in, but I didn't want you to think that I was ignoring you."

Samantha's confused look wasn't surprising, since they weren't exactly friends. "No worries. I didn't even see you, but I'd been craving one of your sister's cupcakes all day."

"They are amazing." A glint of sunlight caught her eye, and Olivia reached down and grabbed Samantha's hand. "Is that a diamond ring?"

Samantha raised her hand to show it off. "Isn't it gorgeous?" she gushed. "Jacob proposed last night!"

Proposed? So she and Jacob *were* together. Maybe Kristy had no idea what she was talking about it. "Congratulations! It is a *gorgeous* ring. Jacob did an excellent job."

"I know," Samantha said, staring down at it. "We wanted to keep things private, especially with Yvette's passing being so recent, but I just can't hide it."

Olivia saw the opening and took it. "I heard that Jacob and Yvette had just gone into business together. That's got to be tough."

"The woman couldn't even be bothered to show up to her own wedding. How reliable of an employee could she be?" Samantha snapped.

Surprised, Olivia blinked and stared. She was just about to point out that one didn't have anything to do with the other when Samantha's shoulders slumped. "I'm sorry. I shouldn't have said that. It's not right to speak ill of the dead, I've just been anxious. Everyone knows about Jacob and Yvette's past, and I'm afraid it will cloud the town's perception when we announce our engagement. I just want everything to be perfect."

Goodwin's ears went up, and he stared at Samantha just as Snowball tried to dart past them and nearly dragged Jackie to the ground. Samantha stiffened and took a step back. Too late, Olivia realized that Samantha had a fear of dogs. "Snowball," Olivia snapped. "Behave."

Rather than do as asked, Snowball simply turned and bounded in the opposite direction. Jackie barely managed to hang on as the giant dog jumped up against a newcomer and proceeded to give him sloppy kisses.

"Hey, Snowball." Jacob laughed. "Olivia. Jackie. Out walking the pups?"

"More like they're walking us," Jackie said dryly.

"What are you ladies talking about?"

Olivia was about to congratulate him on the engagement when Samantha jumped in. "Nothing," she lied. "Just talking about the dogs."

Glancing over her shoulder, Olivia saw Samantha tuck the engagement ring in her pocket. Wow. Jacob really had asked her to keep it a secret. Exactly what was he hiding?

"I've been meaning to talk to you," Jacob said quietly. "I know you found Yvette. That had to be horrible."

"It was shocking. I know that you two were close."

A shadow passed over his face. "We had a good, solid plan for the future. Yvette was already doing great business, but we were going to take it to the next level. I'm only sorry that she won't be around to see it."

"What do you mean? Are you keeping Jump Start open? I thought Yvette was just renting the truck from you."

"She wanted to expand, so she needed an investor. I was that investor. I know that she would want her dream realized, so once a respectable amount of time has passed, I'll start hiring to help carry out our big ideas."

A shadow passed over his face, and Samantha reached out and took his hand. "I'm sure she would have liked that," she said encouragingly.

Goodwin strained at the leash toward Samantha again, and the woman stepped back with a yelp.

Jacob immediately moved between them. "Sorry, Olivia. Samantha was bitten when she was younger and doesn't love being around dogs. Anyway, we should get going. We've got a big night in the city planned."

"Sure," Olivia murmured, and firmly pulled Goodwin aside. Jacob took Samantha's hand and led her away. Waiting until they were out of earshot, Olivia glanced over at Jackie. "Tell me that didn't seem weird to you."

"It is suspicious, but all you can do is take your suspicions to Nick."

"Right," Olivia said with a sigh. "Because I am not getting involved."

"Keep saying it enough times, and maybe you'll actually start to listen to yourself." Jackie handed Olivia Snowball's leash. "I've got to stop by the bookstore for a couple of hours, but I'll be at your place tonight, okay? You better have wine."

"A bottle for each of us," Olivia confirmed, but her mind was already racing. If she went to Nick with this information, she knew what he would say. Right now all she had was a strange feeling. That was hardly worth passing on to Nick. She needed something more concrete.

Proof.

So how exactly was she going to get it?

Chapter Fourteen

Jackie had just finished grilling the chicken for the pasta when Janelle showed up with a dozen fresh-baked cookies. Olivia answered the door with a glass of wine. "I'll trade you," she said immediately, snagging a cookie.

"I'd remind you that we're about to eat dinner, but you could eat all of these cookies and still have room for dinner. Seriously, I have no idea where you put it," Janelle said critically as she grabbed the glass of wine.

Shoving a cookie in her mouth, Olivia grinned. "It'll catch up to me eventually."

"I see you conned Jackie into cooking. At least I know the dinner won't kill me. Patrick is ecstatic that he has the night to himself. I believe he mentioned gambling and debauchery with Andrew."

Olivia snorted. "I doubt Patrick even knows how to gamble, and their idea of debauchery is a six-pack and a Bruce Willis movie."

"That just means that Patrick is going to feel guilty when I have to clean up after him. Date night next week is going to be extra special," Janelle said with a wink.

"Janelle!" Jackie exclaimed as she raised her glass. "This is so long overdue. Seriously, when was the last time we all hung out together, and don't say the town meeting. That cannot possibly count."

"I think it was your birthday," Olivia said with a cock of her head. "Janelle is an old married woman now. She doesn't have time for us single women anymore."

Jackie's face fell. "So when you get married, you're going to leave me too?"

"Don't be ridiculous. I'm not getting married," Olivia baited Janelle. As predicted, her older sister whirled around.

"What? But Andrew . . ." Her voice trailed off when she realized that she had given herself away.

"Andrew what?"

Janelle studied the floor and shrugged. "He's probably going to propose eventually. You two have been together for a year. It's the next step."

Were those her words or his?

"Ladies, why don't we eat, and instead of focusing on your endless problems with amazing men, we can talk about how I'm still single," Jackie interrupted as she pulled down the plates. "And how we're going to fix that, because my nights are filled with fictional men."

Olivia helped her friend serve the chicken pasta. "I could always hook you up with Andrew's friend, Brett. He's yummy, and girl, you are right up his alley."

"Jackie wants someone serious, not a one-night stand," Janelle said with a roll of her eyes. "And you shouldn't be describing other men as yummy."

They sat at the table, and Olivia picked up her fork, took a bite, and closed her eyes in bliss. "Hey, I call it as I see it. Besides, maybe Jackie is just the kind of woman that Brett needs. Someone who doesn't melt at his flowery words and deep-gazing eyes." She sighed, and Jackie and Janelle stared at her. She grabbed at the wine bottle and upended it over her glass, but only a few drops came out.

"I'm sorry, are you trying to set him up with you or me?" Jackie joked.

Olivia was in the middle of opening another wine bottle as she replied. "I wouldn't trade Andrew for the likes of Brett for anything in the world," she admitted. "But that doesn't mean I can't appreciate beauty." She filled her glass and topped off the others' glasses for good measure as the conversation continued.

"When you're married, you can't say things like that," Janelle sniffed.

Both Jackie and Olivia groaned. "Janelle, you're married,

you're not dead. When was the last time that you had some fun?"

Stabbing at her pasta, Janelle scowled. "What are you talking about? I love my life. My job is fun. My husband is fun. My life is fun."

"Those are the words of someone who doesn't have fun," Olivia observed.

"I have to agree," Jackie said as she lifted her glass. "We should do something after dinner."

"After dinner?" Janelle blinked at them as if she had no idea people did stuff after it got dark.

Olivia and Jackie exchanged an amused look.

"We could take Goodwin for a walk by the river," Jackie suggested tentatively, looking from one to the other.

"I said something *fun*, Janelle. Not something that I do three times a day," Olivia said dryly. "Jackie, is this the Velveeta that I bought? It's got green things in it."

"That would be spinach. It's good for you."

"Eh." Olivia frowned and poked at it. "I don't know."

"You eat like you're eight. It's good. Eat the spinach, and we'll let you have cookies later."

"We could go see a movie," Janelle suggested.

Jackie's eyes lit up. "Yes. I haven't seen a movie in forever! Chick flick? Romantic comedy? Horror flick? Oh, let's watch a horror flick."

"Not a horror film," Janelle begged. "I'll have nightmares for weeks."

"Is this spinach even fresh?" Olivia muttered as she pushed it to the side.

"Why are you obsessing about the spinach?"

As her gaze darted around the table, Olivia set her fork down and smiled. Janelle was nice and relaxed, and Jackie was up for anything. It was time for some multi-tasking. Bond with her sister and get the proof that she needed to show Nick. "I know what we can do tonight."

Her admission was met with silence. The other women stared at her, but it was Janelle who spoke first. "Well? Are you going to tell us?"

"I think it would be better if it was a surprise. Trust me, it's something that neither of you ladies have done before. It's time that we shook things up a bit."

"There's nothing in Lexingburg that we haven't done," Jackie pointed out.

Olivia smiled. "Do you trust me?"

"No," Janelle and Jackie said simultaneously.

"I'm hurt," Olivia said with a fake pout. "You're going to be sorry that you said that. I will expect an apology before this evening is over." She gave her friend and sister her brightest smile. "More wine?"

Two hours later, Janelle stared at the building before them. "I thought you didn't want to take Goodwin out for a walk."

"We're not exactly taking him for a walk," Olivia said vaguely.

Jackie crossed her arms. "This is Jacob's condo, and he's not here. What exactly are you planning?"

"Wait, how do you know that Jacob isn't here?" Janelle asked.

"Because we ran into him earlier today, and he told us that he was planning a night out in the city with Samantha. Olivia thinks he killed Yvette."

Janelle gasped. "Olivia! We can't be here! What were you thinking?"

"I was thinking that I can't go to Nick without proof. Jacob isn't going to be here tonight, and we just said that we needed to do something different. This is different."

"By breaking and entering!"

Jackie smirked. "I thought we were going to do something different."

"Wait, you've broken into someone's house before?" Olivia asked with a frown. "When? Why? And more importantly, how was I not involved?"

"That doesn't matter. What matters is that if you do this, you're breaking your promise to Andrew not to get involved."

A couple strolled by them, and the three women immediately shut their mouths. At least they could agree that discussing illegal activity in front of Jacob's neighbors wasn't a good idea. Olivia held Goodwin tightly against her leg. When the coast was clear, she relaxed.

"What's worse? Me breaking my promise to Andrew or having a killer walk the streets of Lexingburg? Besides, it's not breaking and entering because I have a key. And Andrew will forgive me. He doesn't seem to give a damn what I do these days." She said the last part almost under her breath.

"How do you have a key? Jacob doesn't have a dog."

"No, but when he and Yvette were together, they adopted a Beagle together. Yvette took the dog when they split up. I think she gave it to her sister. Anyway, Jacob gave me a key because I was supposed to watch the dog when they went on their honeymoon. I bet you he hasn't changed the locks."

"That was months ago! You never gave him his key back?"

Olivia shrugged. "Honestly, I couldn't figure out the best way to bring the subject up without pouring salt over the wound, and he never asked for it back."

"Let's say that Jacob did kill Yvette," Janelle whispered. "What do you think is going to happen when we walks in on us?"

"He's not. Believe me, Samantha is going to keep him out for half the night. You two wanted some excitement. It doesn't get more exciting than this, except for maybe when Jackie was indulging in her own illegal activity. Now, we can go home like three pathetic wimps, or we can take a few minutes and see if Jacob killed Yvette."

"I am not a wimp," Janelle hissed as she spun on her heel and started marching to the condos.

"Andrew is going to kill you, and then he's going to kill us because we didn't talk you out of it," Jackie muttered.

Olivia felt a wave of pain. "I don't think that Andrew is going to care," she muttered.

They took the elevator up to the third floor where Jacob lived. Jackie and Olivia lounged against one side while Janelle tapped her toe nervously and studied the man sharing the elevator with them. Her bravado when she'd entered the building was rapidly deteriorating as the seconds passed. When she turned back to Olivia, there was nothing but panic in her eyes. Olivia opened her mouth to distract her sister, but it was too late. Janelle was already talking. "We're just going to see our friend," Janelle said in a high pitch. "These are such nice condos. I don't think I've ever been in them before. Do you like living here? Our friend is named Sandy. Do you know Sandy? I bet you and Sandy would really get along well. She's a nurse. Nurse Sandy."

"For the love of . . . Janelle," Olivia hissed. Her sister had a tendency to babble when she was nervous, and she was the worst liar. The more she talked, the crazier she seemed. "Maybe you shouldn't have had that last glass of wine."

Janelle's cheeks reddened and she waved her hand to cool herself off. "Yes. I'm drunk. Please don't listen to anything that I say. Did I mention that we were visiting a friend?"

The stranger gave them a once-over and smiled. "Your friend is lucky." The elevator doors opened, and he stepped out.

"Did he just hit on me? I don't think that he realized I was married," Janelle said with an air of outrage.

"You are so bad at this," Jackie said, shaking her head. "It's all coming back to me now. Every time we got in trouble as kids, it was because you couldn't keep your mouth shut."

"I was supposed to be looking out for you," Janelle reminded her. "Someone has to keep you two in check."

The elevator dinged and the door opened again. Janelle peered nervously around the corner, and Olivia rolled her eyes. "You're not being obvious at all. Come on."

There were four condos per floor. Jacob's was on the left, facing the courtyard. Olivia felt a thrill of satisfaction when the key slid into the hole and turned. "Bingo," she whispered. She opened the door cautiously and turned on the light.

Yvette and Jacob had one thing in common. Jacob's place was spotless. The two-bedroom condo was sparsely decorated. A large television screen hung on the wall, along with pictures from Jacob's high school days. He'd been the star on their football team, and it was obvious that Jacob still relished his golden years. "Did you kill Yvette because she was standing between you and Samantha? Or did you kill her because her business plan didn't fit with yours?"

"What are we looking for?" Jackie whispered.

"See if you can't find the paperwork explaining Yvette's business plan," Olivia muttered as she glanced out the window. "Or anything that would put Jacob at the scene of the crime."

"Jacob owns the food truck. Even if we find something from the truck here, it doesn't prove that Jacob killed Yvette," Jackie pointed out.

174

Olivia shut the curtain and walked into the second bedroom. Jacob had converted it into an office. She shuffled through the papers on the desk and frowned. There was nothing personal in the room, nor was there any evidence of a woman's touch. "Hey, Jackie. Check the bathroom. See if Samantha might be living here, too."

"Does that matter?"

"Call it curiosity," Olivia murmured. Rumors ran rampant in small-town communities, but Kristy had seemed like she'd believed what she was saying. Yvette might not have been the best person, but she wouldn't have done anything with Jacob if she'd known he was with Samantha.

Would she?

"Nothing. No lipstick. No bobby pins. Not even a picture of her," Jackie called back. "That's really strange."

Olivia found the file folder labeled *Jump Start Coffee*. According to the contents, Yvette and Jacob had planned to expand to three trucks. They were going to celebrate the expansion with a food truck festival in Lowell. Pulling out her phone, she looked up the festival. It wasn't until next month, but Yvette's trucks were still slated to attend. "That's a huge expansion," Olivia whispered to herself. Yvette was all about making money, but she really wasn't into putting in the work. What if she hadn't been on board?

"I think I found something," Janelle said hesitantly. "It's Jacob's tablet. If he has a calendar on his phone, won't it sync to the tablet?"

"Good thinking," Olivia said excitedly as she put the folder back and shut the drawer. "You're good at this, Janelle."

Olivia opened the magnetic flap and smirked when she saw the tablet wasn't password-protected. Opening the calendar app, she scrolled through his appointments. "Wow, Jacob has been a busy boy. Tiki's Tacos and Submarine, those are the other two food trucks that Franklin had, right? He's had a lot of appointments with them. If he's being this aggressive with Jump Start, he might be planning on expanding these as well."

"Makes sense," Janelle said with a shrug. "Franklin doesn't always have great things to say about Jacob. He's probably trying to prove that he's as business savvy as his father."

"T.T. It looks like he was meeting with Tiki's Tacos the morning that Yvette was killed." Olivia's shoulders slumped. "That's a pretty solid alibi. It might be why Nick's not investigating him."

"I'd say that someone should double-check that alibi," Jackie said as she emerged from the bedroom. "Look what I found in his underwear drawer."

"What were you doing in his underwear drawer?" Janelle

gasped.

"Looking for clues." Jackie waggled her eyebrows. "He's a boxers kind of guy, if you're interested."

Olivia closed the tablet and handed it back to Janelle. "Okay, you seriously need a boyfriend. What did you find?"

"It's a copy of Jacob's contract with Yvette. He said that he invested in her business, but according to this, if she didn't pay him back within six months, he could take control of her business. There isn't any way that she could have paid him back in time. There's no way that Yvette read this before she signed it. No one would have agreed to this."

"And he's obviously trying to hide it," Olivia murmured as she glanced over it. "If Yvette discovered this, she would have freaked out."

"It could have been a crime of passion, but what are the chances that Jacob's act of vengeance was long-term? She left him at the altar, so he took the only thing that she cared about. All that talk of expanding her business was just a lure to con her into signing it over to him," Olivia murmured.

"But he has an alibi," Jackie pointed out.

"He has an appointment. That's hardly concrete." Olivia pulled out her phone and snapped a picture of the contract.

"How are you going to explain to Nick how you got this?" Jackie asked with a frown.

"Anonymous tip," Olivia said with a smile. "He never has to know that it was me."

"You're not going to tell Andrew, are you?" Janelle accused.

"You tell Patrick where you were tonight, and I'll tell Andrew," Olivia said with a sly smile.

Janelle sighed in displeasure. "You so owe me for this."

Olivia smiled. "Maybe I'll buy you some new pipes."

CHAPTER FIFTEEN

Rose fingered the key in her hands and stared at the box. All the documents, all the files—nothing but a wild goose chase. Was it possible that the necklace had been here the whole time? The gold-painted design was faded. She ran her fingers over it and smiled. It was the same design as the one doodled on the letter her grandmother had written to her grandfather, leading the reader to believe that she'd gotten a safety deposit box.

Clever old woman. She'd known that the neighbors were sniffing around.

Turning the box over, Rose ran her fingers over the edge until she found the groove. Sliding the small wood panel aside, she inserted the key into the hidden lock.

The top popped open, and the soft melody of a lullaby filled the air. Slowly lifting the top, she held her breath, seeing the navy blue leather pouch revealed inside. As she pulled it out, her mind flashed back to the only memory she'd ever had of the necklace. Her grandmother and her father had been arguing over it. Her father wanted it sold to pay for something that he wanted, but her grandmother had insisted that it was Rose's legacy.

Now, after all this time, she'd finally have it. "Thank you Mama," she whispered. "Thank you."

As she opened the pouch, she heard the familiar click of a cocked gun. "I knew you would find it," a dark voice said. "All I had to do was wait. Hand it over, Rose."

"You."

"Olivia? Hello! Earth to Olivia!"

Annoyed at the interruption, Olivia paused her audiobook and couldn't help glaring before she was able to compose her features into a neutral expression. "Mayor Henderson," she said with a sigh. "How can I help you?" She was walking Lily and Goodwin through the town square that morning. The dachshund sniffed at Douglas and started attempting to climb up his leg.

"Off!" Douglas said with a shudder. "Control your beasts, Olivia."

"Lily!" she chastised as she snapped her fingers and gently pulled the dog off. "Is there something that you needed?"

Douglas sniffed and reached up to straighten his toupee. "I would like to hire you."

"Hire me?" Olivia repeated, confused. "Mayor, I'm a dog walker. You don't have a dog."

"I do now. I went into Lowell and adopted one yesterday. He's called Bender or Fender or something. I'll need you to walk him three times a day. Maybe four. I'm not certain how many times dogs should be walked."

"You got a dog?" Unable to help herself, Olivia looked around to see if anyone else was witnessing the conversation. "I don't mean offense, Mayor Henderson, but you don't even like dogs. You certainly shouldn't have one if you need to hire me to take care of it full time."

"I like dogs," Douglas snapped. "I love dogs, but I'm a busy man—so, are you going to help me or not?"

"You don't love dogs," Olivia laughed. "You love . . . Celeste." Understanding dawned. "Of course you got a dog. Celeste loves dogs, and you wanted a chance to talk to her. Mayor Henderson, I can commend you on adopting a dog—but you're better off just talking to Celeste."

"I don't know what you're talking about. I have no such feelings toward Celeste," Douglas denied. "And I can see that you're not professional enough to help me. No worries. There are plenty of dog walkers in Lowell who would be more than happy to take me on as a client. I am the mayor, after all."

Olivia fought against the urge to rub her temples. She had a headache. After they'd gotten home from Jacob's the night before, Janelle had kept them up even later by fretting about what would happen if they got caught. She attempted to force Olivia and Jackie to take a blood oath, swearing their silence. But Olivia just poured her sister another couple of glasses of wine and convinced her that they'd already done it. Her sister was practically asleep when Olivia drove her to her house—and wouldn't be able to say a single thing.

Too tired to try to get the mayor to see reason, Olivia just sighed. "I would be more than happy to take care of Fender Bender for you, Mayor Henderson. How about I stop by this afternoon and meet the dog, and we can work out a schedule." Privately, she thought to herself that Douglas could stand to take the dog on a few walks himself and lose a couple of pounds, but she had a feeling that mentioning that wouldn't go over well.

"Excellent! And since you brought up Celeste, please let her know that I'd like to include Fender in her sessions. For all I know, the poor dog was abused in his past. I'd like her to communicate with the dog and learn as much as she can about my new companion."

"Of course you would," she muttered with mock sympathy. "I'm sure that she'll be thrilled."

"I'll see you this afternoon, then. Perhaps you could bring some of your sister's cupcakes when you come. Perhaps a dozen of those Oreo ones. I'm fond of those." Smacking his lips, Douglas rubbed his belly and started to whistle as he walked past her. Goodwin whined and looked up at her as if he understood how she was feeling.

"What do you think, Goodwin? Do you think the whole town would benefit if we just told Celeste how Douglas felt about her?"

Goodwin's whine turned into a sharp bark. Olivia immediately recognized an alarm when she heard it and whirled around. A car was careening around the corner of Main Street and Seventh. Frowning, Olivia tugged Lily's leash until the dachshund was back on the sidewalk, but rather than slowing down, the car seemed to pick up speed.

When it jumped the curb and came barreling straight for her, Olivia screamed and started to run with the dogs. If she ducked to the right, she'd get pinned against the buildings, and she wasn't about to risk the lives of the dogs. Too terrified to look back to see how far away the car was, she dove head-first behind the brick *Welcome to Lexingburg* sign and pulled the dogs up close to her. Luckily, the driver seemed to realize that he or she couldn't drive over the sign and veered sharply back onto the street.

Ignoring the pain that lanced up her ankle, Olivia jumped up and craned to see the license plate of the fast-receding car. Black SUV. VLA6027.

Repeating the license plate over and over in her head, she slumped against the sign and took a deep, shuddering breath. Lily's whole body trembled as she tried to climb up Olivia's leg, and Goodwin whined and sniffed her as if to make sure that everyone was okay.

183

Did Jacob realize that she'd gone into his house yesterday? Had he just tried to kill her?

*   *   *

Andrew felt his heart jump in his chest when he saw Olivia sitting in the chair at the sheriff's department. She had a long, ugly scrape down one arm, and she was holding a bag of ice on her ankle. Goodwin and Lily rested on the floor by her chair.

Sitting at his desk across from her, Nick was trying to talk calmly to her, but the mayor kept interrupting them loudly. "I'm telling you, that car just tried to run me over! I was just talking to Olivia, and the next thing I know, the car was heading straight for us!"

"Mayor Henderson," Nick said with a sigh. "You were a couple of blocks away when the incident happened. I don't think that you were the target."

"How can you say that? Why would anyone want to run Olivia over?"

Nick trained a hard look at Olivia. "That's an excellent question. Why would someone want to run you over?"

"They wouldn't," Douglas interjected. "I'm cracking down on crime in Lexingburg, and the criminals are clearly reacting out of

184

fear. Where is the press? This is headline news!"

"Mayor Henderson, Lexingburg isn't exactly teeming with crime," Nick pointed out.

Douglas threw up his hands in disgust. "How can you say that? We just had a high-profile murder, and now someone tried to run me over! I expect you to find this driver and bring them to justice. This takes priority over your other cases, Nick. I'm going to talk to the reporters. Keep me updated!"

"I'm fine, thanks for asking," Olivia called out as Douglas swept past Andrew. Her eyes landed on her boyfriend and widened. "Andrew! What are you doing here?"

"Nick called me," Andrew said, fighting to find his calm center. "You were targeted in a hit-and-run. You could have seriously been hurt. You could have *died*, Olivia."

"I know that, Andrew. I was there," she pointed out as she reached down to stroke Goodwin's head. "But I'm fine, so you can go back to work. If I wasn't fine, I'd be at the hospital."

Andrew narrowed his eyes and walked forward to kneel down next to her. When he reached for her, she gasped, and his hand stilled briefly before he gently probed her ankle. "It could be sprained, sweetheart. I'd feel better if you went to the hospital and had it x-rayed."

"It's fine. I'll try to stay off it for the rest of the day," she muttered, avoiding his gaze.

"I'll call Janelle and Jackie and see if they can't cover your shifts for today and tomorrow. And I'll pick up a brace and some crutches from the hospital," Andrew said as he stood.

"That's not necessary," Olivia protested.

He ignored her. "Nick, who would do this?"

The sheriff shook his head. "With the mayor panicking, I haven't been able to get much information from Olivia other than the vehicle description. It was reported stolen this morning, so that's not very helpful. Olivia, is there a reason that someone would want to run you over?"

Olivia bit her bottom lip, and Andrew's gaze sharpened. It was a telltale sign that she was about to lie. "I don't know, Sheriff. As far as I know, all of my customers are happy."

"I don't think that you were nearly killed because someone is dissatisfied with your dog-walking capabilities," Nick pointed out. "And the fact that you just called me Sheriff rather than Nick is disconcerting. What are you hiding?"

"I'm just trying to be respectful," Olivia protested, and her fingers tightened on the arm of the chair. "And I don't have any proof that someone would want to kill me."

Andrew lifted an eyebrow. "I should think the car that came barreling at you on Main Street would be proof."

Olivia's eyes flickered up and then down again to the dogs as she averted her gaze. "What I mean to say is that I don't know anyone specific who would want to kill me."

"I'll take generic," Nick said. He leaned back and studied her. "Vague. A seedling of an idea. Damn it, Olivia, are you still meddling in this case with Yvette?"

"I did find the body. I'm fairly certain that means I'm already involved," Olivia muttered, continuing to examine the dogs closely.

"What were you doing last night?" Nick asked with narrowed eyes. "Where did you go?"

"I was with Janelle and Jackie last night! We had dinner. We had a girls' night!" she exclaimed.

"That's true," Andrew sighed. "I was with Patrick last night. Olivia had to drop Janelle off because she'd had too much to drink."

Nick shook his head. "Maybe I should make you stay with Janelle until this whole thing is over. At least I know that she has some sense in her head and will keep you out of trouble."

"Someone just tried to run me over—and yet *I'm* the one in

trouble. How is that even fair?" Olivia argued. She wrapped the leashes around her undamaged arm and stood tentatively. Andrew could see the flash of pain in her eyes, but she was a trouper. "I'm sure I'll be fine tomorrow if you want me to walk Tucker. You know, without your wife finding out."

Andrew almost snorted at Olivia's attempt to threaten Nick. "It's okay," he said to Nick. "I'll take her home and make sure that she stays out of trouble for the rest of the day."

"Fine," Nick sighed. "Olivia, if you know something, you have to tell me."

"Sure," she squeaked. "Will do."

Frustrated, Andrew took the leashes from her and put an arm around her as she hobbled out. He couldn't even begin to explain to her how terrified he'd been when Nick had called him and told him that someone had tried to run Olivia down.

Run her down! He'd told her over and over again to stay away from this case because he was terrified that she'd get in too deep and get hurt. Now he was practically half-carrying her out of the sheriff's office.

As he helped her into his car, she gave him a nervous look. "Andrew," she said in a small voice. "Are you mad?"

Leaning over, he kissed her forehead. "You're a victim, Olivia.

Let's get Lily dropped off so I can take you home."

"Andrew," she whispered. "Home first, babe."

He turned on the radio, but she already pulling out her phone. He expected her to fit her ear buds in her ears, but instead, he followed her gaze to the huge crack in her screen. When she moaned, he knew it wasn't in physical pain.

Mentally, he wrestled with what he should do now. The fastest way to push Olivia away was to put a leash on her and demand that she quit this infernal investigation—and that was the last thing that he wanted to do, but he also wanted to keep her safe.

After dropping the dachshund off, he helped Olivia into the house and got her settled on the couch. Grabbing a small stack of books from the top of her "want to read" pile, he laid them down next to her along with the remote to the television. "I'll call Jackie and Janelle and get them to cover your dogs for this afternoon and tonight."

"Thanks," she murmured.

"Olivia, I hope that you realize what you're doing is dangerous. Let Nick handle it."

She flashed him a small smile. "Don't worry. This is a wake-up call."

Praying that it was true, he called in to work and told them he wasn't coming in for the rest of the day, today or tomorrow. Then, he called Jackie and Janelle to cover Olivia's shifts, but all he told them was that she wasn't feeling well. There was no reason to get them roped in as well.

When he returned to Olivia, she was already asleep. Gently, he brushed her hair away from her cheek.

"What am I going to do with you, babe?"

CHAPTER SIXTEEN

Andrew was asleep next to Olivia when she woke up the next morning. She barely remembered moving from the couch to the bed in a haze of pain and exhaustion last night. At least, she thought it had been last night. Everything was a blur. As the sun filtered over his handsome face, she propped herself up on her good elbow and stared at him. She always loved waking up first. It was the only time she got to simply admire him without him asking her why she was staring.

Sometimes she thought it was impossible to express how much she loved him, and other times she knew it would be impossible to express how much she wanted to strangle him.

She'd had no idea that Nick would call him yesterday after Jacob had tried to run her down. Olivia had expected him to call Janelle. She'd even feared that he might call her mother—but Andrew? But it wasn't horror she'd felt when she saw him. It was pleasure. Relief. She didn't even realize, until she saw him, that he was the person that she most wanted to see.

He should have been furious. He knew that she'd put herself in danger because she hadn't dropped Yvette's case, and she'd expected him to yell and threaten, but he'd just kissed her and helped her home. What did that even mean?

191

She should have told Nick what she suspected about Jacob, but she couldn't do it without admitting that she, Jackie, and Janelle had snuck into the man's condo the night before. The only smart thing she could do now was to call in the tip anonymously and hope that Nick caught Jacob before he tried to kill her again. This was all her fault—she shouldn't have kept digging. She should have just left it to Nick. But then she'd have to face the music with Andrew. She'd have to deal with a proposal.

She hated herself for not being able to deal with change.

She decided right then to drop any further meddling—Andrew was too important to lose.

She'd somehow get the final evidence to Nick, and then she'd stop.

A few things still didn't add up. How did Jacob know? There hadn't been any sign of Jacob or Samantha when they'd left the condo last night. Did Jacob have some sort of security that she hadn't seen? If so, why hadn't he turned them in?

When she'd thrown herself to the ground yesterday, she must have landed on her phone because the screen was cracked to bits. Careful not to disturb Andrew, she slowly reached across and snagged his phone from the nightstand. Slipping out of bed, she tested her weight on her ankle. It ached a little, but there was no sharp pain. Thankful that she could resume business as usual, she tiptoed out of the bedroom. Goodwin followed her, and Olivia quietly closed the door behind them.

Dialing Jackie's number, she let Goodwin out and started a pot of coffee. Jackie answered almost on the first ring. "Olivia? I tried to text you, but you didn't respond. Andrew called and said that you weren't feeling well. Are you okay?"

"Nick didn't call you?" Olivia asked in surprise.

"No, why would he? Olivia, what did you do now?"

Of course Jackie would assume that she'd done something. "I'm not to blame here! Someone tried to run me over yesterday morning, and I hurt my ankle. I'm fine now, so I'll be able to do my rounds with the dogs today, but I wasn't sure if you told Nick that we were at Jacob's condo the other night."

"No, he didn't call. I'm sure if he asked Janelle, she would have called me, so our secret is safe. At least for now. Olivia, are you suggesting that Jacob just tried to murder you? We need to tell Nick!"

"I'm going to call the tip line today, so Nick should at least take a good hard look at Jacob. Listen, I broke my phone yesterday, so if you need to get a hold of me, call Andrew. I'm going to go into the city today and see if I can't get a new one. I was *this* close to finishing my book, too."

"You almost die, and the only thing you're concerned about is that you can't finish your book?" Jackie sighed. "Whoa, hold on. Have you seen the newspaper? The headline states that 'Mayor Almost Dies Cracking Down on Crime.' Was he there?"

Olivia moaned. "I almost forgot. He went and adopted a dog in an attempt to get Celeste's attention. He wants me to walk it. He was several blocks away when the car tried to run me over, and he's certain the car was meant for him, and I was just the innocent bystander."

"Really? That poor dog. Someone just needs to tell her. In fact, I think you should do that during your little pet psychic segment today."

"That's today? I almost forgot. Maybe I can convince her that I'm in too much pain."

"She'll just postpone it. You might as well get it over with today."

"Olivia?" Andrew asked huskily behind her. "How is your ankle?"

"Oh—Andrew is up," Olivia said frantically. "I'll need you to call Nick."

"Me?" Jackie gasped. "You didn't tell Andrew? You're the worst . . ."

Olivia hung up before Jackie could finish that accusation. Turning around, she gave Andrew a brilliant smile. "Sorry I snagged your phone. I broke mine yesterday. I wanted to let Jackie know that I can walk the dogs today. Are you going to work?"

"Coffee," was all he rasped as he reached for the pot. Andrew wasn't the best morning person. It was the only time he didn't seem completely in control.

After a few sips of the elixir of life, he leaned against the counter and studied her. "You're limping a little."

"It just aches. Really, I'm fine."

"Are you ready to tell me what you, Jackie, and Janelle really did that night?" Stunned, she just stared at him. Apparently watching her limp around had knocked sleep's haze right out of him. "I know you, Olivia. You think you know who killed Yvette, and the only reason that you didn't tell Nick yesterday was because you, Jackie, and Janelle did something that you shouldn't have done."

"You're too smart for your own good," she grumbled.

"Nick isn't going to arrest Jackie because he's terrified of her, and he isn't going to arrest Janelle because he likes her cookies too much."

"What about me?" she complained as she spread her arms out.

"Do you want Nick to arrest me?"

"It would certainly keep you safe." His gaze intensified. "Tell me the truth."

After pouring her own cup of coffee, she hobbled over to the rug, which would be warmer under her feet than the bare wooden floor. Explaining how she had run into Jacob and Samantha, she went into details about what she and the other two had done and what they'd found. It was almost fascinating to see all the blood drain from Andrew's face.

"You broke into Jacob's condo?" he repeated hoarsely.

"I had a key," she insisted. "Why does no one get that?"

"Nick is looking into Jacob, Olivia. The other night when I didn't come over? Nick asked me to look into Yvette's computer."

Annoyed, she pursed her lips. "So you can help Nick, but I can't?"

"I looked at a computer, Olivia. You broke into a man's home."

"I had a key! Never mind. What did you find?"

"Jacob wasn't at Tiki's Tacos at the time of the murder. According to Franklin, they were together discussing a business strategy. It seemed like a pretty solid alibi, except that Jacob claimed there was nothing between him and Yvette—but there were pictures of their romantic interludes from as recent as a few weeks ago, and there were some deleted files that showed that Jacob was accusing Yvette of skirting commitment."

"Maybe she wasn't skirting commitment. Maybe she realized that Jacob was out for vengeance, and she was biding her time. After all, he owned the truck, and she needed his investment money. Maybe she knew all along that it wasn't real."

"What makes you think it wasn't real?"

"He proposed to Samantha! She said it's supposed to be a secret, but she's sporting a huge rock on her finger. You don't date one woman and then propose to another less than a week after her death. Jacob isn't that cold."

"Really? You're talking about a man you suspect of spending nearly a year planning his revenge. What's to say that he didn't propose to Samantha to throw off suspicion that he'd had a fling with Yvette? Let me see the picture of the contract."

"I can't. My phone is broken, remember?"

"No worries. Everything is backed up wirelessly to your computer." He sat his cup down and went to grab her laptop off the coffee table. A few minutes later, he'd pulled up her photos.

"Do you check that often?" she asked curiously.

"Why?" he asked with a smirk. "Are you hiding something from

197

me?"

"Just my other boyfriends. Carlos. And Ivan."

"A Latino and a Russian?" Andrew cocked his head. "Interesting mix."

"Don't worry," she teased. "You're my favorite. It should be the last photo that I took."

"Here we go," he muttered as he pulled up the blurry picture. "Sweetheart, we really need to work on your photography skills." He read silently for a few moments, his brow furrowed, then said, "Yeah, this is not a standard contract. Andrew's lawyers made it as complicated as possible so that even if she did read it, she probably didn't understand it. I'll let Nick know to get in touch with the lawyers and pull up the other contracts he has with the food trucks to see if they're similar."

"And when he asks how you got the information?"

"He's not going to ask because he's not going to want the details. After that, we're done. No more investigating for us."

"Fine."

"Fine?" he repeated skeptically.

"Yes," Olivia said, trying to keep the irritation out of her voice.

He closed the laptop and laid it aside. "Now, are you sure that you want to walk the dogs today?"

"I told you, I'm fine. Go to work."

"I'm not going to work. I am going to stick fairly close to you today—just in case—plus, I'm dying to see what Celeste is going to say to Goodwin today."

Olivia glared at him. "I swear, this whole town hates me."

An hour later, she had Tucker, Lily, Snowball, Goodwin, and an ancient Basset Hound with *Fender* written in Sharpie across his yellow collar. "Douglas called this dog a Beagle," Olivia said in an outraged voice. "He has no business having this dog."

Andrew frowned as he stared at the slow-moving dog. "I don't think you have anything to worry about. The dog looks like he isn't going to live long enough to see tomorrow, let alone live long enough for Douglas to do any damage to him."

"Shh," Olivia whispered. "He'll hear you."

He shook his head. "Nope. I don't think that dog can hear anything."

He wasn't wrong. Fender ignored every command that Olivia tried, and she was pretty certain that he couldn't see out of his right eye. Every time he turned his head, he yelped as though he was surprised to see the other dogs.

To compensate for Fender's age, they were walking so slowly that a snail could have passed them. Snowball whined in frustration and pulled at the leash, but the other dogs seemed happy enough to walk slowly and sniff everything. As they passed the empty spot that used to house Jump Start, Olivia gazed at it uneasily.

It seemed that the more she found out about Yvette, the less she realized she knew about the woman. There had been a time when she'd admired the woman. Yvette did what she wanted when she wanted. She didn't need to put down roots. Even her job was mobile, but now that she was dead, Olivia realized Yvette had been nothing but a lonely woman who'd died without any friends. In fact, the one man who'd loved her ended up hating her.

What would happen if Olivia turned Andrew down? Would he grow to hate her? Would she end up like Yvette?

Fender stopped suddenly and started nosing around in the bushes. Olivia was so lost in her anxiety that she didn't even realize what the Basset Hound was doing until he was halfway under the bush. "Fender!" she said sharply and tugged on the leash. Slowly, the dog wobbled out, his jaws working. "No, spit it out! Whatever is in your mouth, spit it out now! Drop it!"

When the dog didn't move to obey any of her orders, she crouched down and pried the dog's jaws open. Snagging the object that was in his mouth, she pulled it out, along with a long line of drool. "Disgusting," she muttered as she held the ring up. The sunlight sparkled off the gem. "It's an emerald!"

Andrew staggered suddenly, slapped his hand to his heart, and gave a loud, dramatic sigh. "Olivia! Of course I will marry you! I love you so much, although next time, maybe shoot for a diamond? I'm a pretty traditional guy."

Unable to help herself, she laughed. "I'd have to get it resized. It's much too small for you." She wiped the slobber off and peered at it for closer inspection. "I recognize the design. I think this is one of Stanley Gems' rings. I'll take it to him and see if he can remember who he sold it to. I'm sure someone is missing it."

"We'll stop by after your meeting with Celeste. I think the whole town has been talking about this," Andrew teased.

Groaning, Olivia pocketed the ring. It was time to face the music.

CHAPTER SEVENTEEN

As it turned out, Andrew hadn't been joking. There were so many people gathered around Celeste's little shop that the lady herself had set up shop outside. There was a small table outside the building covered in a red tablecloth, with her signature crystal ball in the middle. Celeste herself wore a red dress with a variety of dogs printed on it and a scarf that matched.

Olivia noted that although Douglas was in the crowd, he wasn't trying to draw attention to himself. The only time that the mayor was shy was around Celeste.

"Olivia!" Lady Celeste greeted, using her dramatically low-pitched stage voice. "I'm so glad that you could make it, and you brought me so many lovely dogs. I'm so excited to get to know these pooches better," she said as she crouched down to let the dogs kiss her.

Andrew handed Olivia his leashes and stepped back into the crowd. To her horror, he pulled out his phone and trained it on her.

"You are not filming this!" she whispered in alarm.

"Relax, sweetheart. This could be your big break!"

Olivia sighed, but on further thought, couldn't help but chuckle. Despite the ridiculous situation she was in, she was in a good mood. Soon Jacob would be in custody, and she could finally put

Yvette's murder behind her. She'd started to see Janelle as a sister again and felt more comfortable helping her out. Even she and Andrew were having a good time despite his impending proposal hanging over her head.

For the first time in a long time, she was starting to feel like herself again.

"Let's start with Goodwin, shall we?" Celeste took Goodwin's leash and led him back to the table. Goodwin was such a happy dog that he didn't even think twice about Celeste putting her hands all over him. "Olivia, why don't you tell our audience a few things about Goodwin?"

Olivia cleared her throat and glanced around nervously. She wasn't great in large crowds. "Well, as many of you know, I adopted Goodwin a couple of years ago from the shelter. There isn't much that we know about him, but the vet approximates that he's about three years old and that he's probably a mix between wolfhound, mastiff, and Lab. He prefers Andrew . . ."

"As do most of us!" someone from the crowd shouted. Everyone, including Olivia, laughed.

". . . and he's quite the thief when it comes to food. He's fond of sausage pizza and scrambled eggs, and he thinks that cats are out to take over the world."

"Yes," Celeste murmured. "Now, as you probably realize, dogs don't think like we do, but they recognize certain words. I could feel Goodwin's displeasure when he heard his mistress mention the word cat. Ah, there it is again. I feel that there was an unpleasant experience in his past with a cat, but Goodwin has a loving soul, and I'm sure he could learn to at least tolerate another cat so long as he felt that his mistress and his master still loved and protected him. Yes, you love your Olivia and Andrew, don't you?"

To Olivia's surprise, Goodwin put his paw up on Celeste's knee as though he understood her. Celeste probably had some treats hidden in her pockets. That was how he acted when he wanted treats.

"Do you have a specific question that you want me to ask him?" Celeste asked with a smile.

"I guess I'd like to know where he keeps hiding my socks. I swear he steals a pair a week." The crowd tittered with laughter, and even Celeste laughed. She slowly massaged the dog's head and whispered to him. After a few minutes, she lifted her head. "Does Goodwin have a crate with a gray bed inside it?"

Stunned, Olivia slowly nodded her head. Celeste smiled with satisfaction. "I believe you'll find your socks under his bed."

"Wow. I will definitely check," Olivia muttered as she stepped forward and grabbed Goodwin's leash. She was thoroughly impressed, but that didn't mean that Celeste hadn't asked around for personal details about Olivia and Goodwin. She was about to hand over Tucker's leash when there was the loud sound of throat-clearing. Rolling her eyes, Olivia separated Fender's leash instead. "Lady Celeste, this is Fender. Fender is the very brand-spanking-new member of Mayor Henderson's family. I would suggest that you ask Fender why Mayor Henderson felt like he needed to get a dog."

If Celeste understand what Olivia was insinuating, she ignored it. "Oh, Fender," she gushed. "You are a gorgeous animal, and you've lived a full life, haven't you?" To Olivia, she said, "I can tell that things are a bit muted and a little fuzzy for him. He's deaf, yes? And his vision is impaired?"

"Based on the half an hour that I've spent with him this morning, I suspect that he's blind in one eye and hard of hearing. He also seems to be attracted to sparkling things."

"Yes," Celeste whispered as she laid a hand over the dog's eye. "I can see that. Fender has been very loved—and experienced a recent and devastating loss. I believe his previous owner passed away, poor fellow. But his life has been full of salty air, warm sand, hikes in the mountains, and . . ." Her voice trailed off, and then she nodded and added, "boating. I believe Fender is a well-traveled pup. What a lucky boy he is! Mayor Henderson, do you have a specific question that you'd like me to ask him?"

"Whatever you want to ask him is fine," Douglas spluttered

nervously.

"I have a question for him. Perhaps you could ask what commands he knows, because he doesn't seem to understand sit, stay, lay down, or drop," Olivia volunteered. "Maybe he speaks a different language."

The crowd laughed softly, but Celeste was already concentrating on Fender. "Hmm, it would seem that he does understand *drop*, but he liked the ring because it tasted like coffee. It seems that Fender is very fond of coffee."

Coffee? "Wait, what did you just say?" Olivia demanded.

"Okay," Andrew said as he stepped forward. "Lady Celeste, that is an amazing demonstration, but I'm sure some of these other lovely people are eager for your assistance. We'll bring Tucker, Lily, and Snowball back another time. I would love to discover how Snowball feels about his little costumes." He took Fender's leash and handed it to Douglas.

"Andrew," she whispered urgently. "Did you hear Celeste?"

"I did, and before that overactive imagination of yours gets you in trouble, remember that before that very second, you believed Celeste was a fraud," he reminded her as he led her away from the crowd.

"Okay, but Goodwin does have a crate with a gray bed."

"Yes, I know, darling. I also know that you've posted about a million photos of Goodwin in his crate on social media."

"Okay, but how would she know about the ring?"

"I'm sure someone saw us."

Blowing out her breath in frustration, Olivia reached up and grabbed his arm. "Andrew, stop. Can't we at least go to Stanley's now and show him the ring? If it does end up belonging to Yvette, we'll hand it over to Nick."

He studied her for a long a moment, and Olivia was sure that he was finally about to put his foot down. Instead, he just pursed his lips and shook his head. "We'll drop off the dogs, and then we'll go," he said with a sigh. "But if it turns out to be nothing, I want you to drop it. Promise?"

"I promise."

CHAPTER EIGHTEEN

It didn't occur to Olivia until after she'd entered the store that the reason Andrew could have been so reluctant to visit Stanley's was because he'd commissioned their engagement ring from him. Lowell had jewelers, of course, but they were chain stores with no heart. However, when they entered the small store, which sat a few streets back from the town square, Andrew didn't look particularly concerned.

Stanley's Gems might be an expensive jewelry store, but it housed everything from costume jewelry to large sparkly diamonds. There was a small corner section with plastic tiaras and colored glass, probably where Snowball's owners got his sparkly decorations, but there were also glass display cases with gorgeous and expensive-looking gems. Diamonds, sapphires, rubies, pearls.

And emeralds.

Stanley's daughter, Julie, stood behind the counter and gave them a wide smile. "Welcome to Stanley's," she greeted them cheerfully. "You two look like a couple in love. What are we looking for today? A gift for a special occasion? Anniversary? Engagement, perhaps?"

Finally, someone who didn't know that Andrew was supposed to be proposing to her. Giving him a sly side look to gauge his expression, she was disappointed to see his face was still impassive. It would be so much easier to discuss the engagement before the proposal if she didn't have to give away that she already knew about the whole thing. "None of the above. We found this ring on the sidewalk this morning, and we wanted to return it to the owner."

Julie immediately pulled out her jeweler's loupe to examine the ring. "I see that it doesn't have an inscription," she murmured. Putting the loupe down, she shook her head. "We can inscribe even the thinnest bands, you know. Initials or a simple 'I love you.' It can make all the difference in the world."

Olivia exchanged an amused look with Andrew. "We'll be sure to spread the word," she assured her. It seemed that while Stanley was the designer, his daughter was the sales woman. They made a dynamic team.

"That's so sweet of you!" Julie beamed as she went back to examining the ring. "It's an emerald, beautiful color and stunning clarity. Just a little under two carats. Platinum setting. If I remember the design correctly, this ring had two small diamonds that were supposed to sit on either side of the emerald. It's a shame that they're missing. I'm sure the owner is more than anxious to get them replaced, which we do here without a fee for the first five years."

"Yes, I'm sure they're very anxious. Did your father make this ring in the past five years?" Olivia prodded her.

"I don't think that it was a special order," Julie said, handing the ring back. "And I'm afraid that I don't remember the sale, but I think we must have featured this ring in our design catalogue because it's simply stunning. If that's true, then it'll be possible to link the catalogue number with the purchaser, assuming that they used a credit card."

Olivia had been just about to thank the woman when Julie reached under and pulled out a huge three-ring binder. It hit the counter hard, and she pushed it their way. "Okay. If you find it, please let me know."

Olivia stared at the book in dismay, then looked up at Andrew. It would seem that Julie was much less interested in them now that she realized they weren't here to buy. "I think we're going to be here for a while."

He kissed the top of her head. "Why don't you finish up here, and I'll run into the city and get you a replacement phone. I want to make sure that I get there before the store closes."

A replacement phone meant that she'd finally be able to discover who was after Rose's necklace. "That would be amazing, thank you."

"If it does link back to Yvette, you'll take the ring straight to Nick?"

"Scout's honor!" she promised.

"Okay." He sauntered out the door, and she clutched the binder to her chest and sat down heavily on one of the chairs by the wall. Her ankle still ached a little, and she needed a break.

The book wasn't the most organized. Olivia had hoped that it was, at the very least, divided by gemstone, but it wasn't. As she slowly flipped through the book, she couldn't help but let a forbidden question pop into her head.

What kind of ring had Andrew gotten her? Did he think that she was the princess-cut type or maybe the dainty teardrop? Was it a gold band or silver? While Olivia didn't wear much jewelry, she had a whole stand crammed full of jewelry that she'd collected over the years. Some pieces were from ex-boyfriends who'd refused to take them back. Most were impulse buys that she'd purchased herself but never wore, a mix of metals and colors. One spring, Olivia had gone crazy over mint-green stones, and that winter, she'd obsessed over black pearls.

There were moments when she wanted to be girly. Despite her chef coat, Janelle was always impeccably dressed underneath. Even Jackie, in her own quirky way, managed to seem feminine and gorgeous. Olivia was never like that. When she looked at women liked Delilah, she wondered why Andrew had chosen her. She wanted to wear perfect makeup and deck herself out in shiny baubles, but those moments were few and far-between.

A customer entered the store, reminding Olivia of her mission.

She went back to flipping through the book until, what seemed like hours later, she finally discovered what she was looking for.

There it was—the deep green emerald popped out in the photo, sparkling on what was probably Julie's perfectly manicured finger. Holding her place with her hand, Olivia hurried back up to the counter to get Julie's attention, laid the binder down and pointed to the photo of the ring.

"Did you find it?" Julie asked with loud enthusiasm. "Yes, you did! You're such a good detective!" She was using almost the same voice that Olivia used when praising Goodwin, but it wasn't the tone that bothered Olivia. It was the praise itself.

Olivia furrowed her brow. "Detective?" Did Julie know what she was doing?

"Yes! You're taking the time to hunt down the owner of this ring. Putting your nose to the ground and sniffing out clues! I'll just take this design number to the back and see if I can't find who purchased it." With a bright smile, Julie practically bounced to the back room. Briefly, Olivia wondered how much coffee the woman had to drink in order to have that much energy.

Left alone with the other customer in the store, Olivia looked over at him and gave him a weak smile. "Hi," she said lamely. "I'm not really doing any detective work. I kind of promised my boyfriend that I wouldn't. He worries about me. I'm just trying to return a ring."

"You didn't like the ring?" he asked.

"Oh, no. I'm not returning it here. I'm returning it to its owner. It's not an engagement ring. At least, it's not my engagement ring. I found it. But my boyfriend has a ring. At least, I assume that he has a ring. I'm sure I'll love it. It's not like I'm the kind of woman who would turn down a proposal because I don't like the ring. No, I would turn down the proposal because I'm not sure he's asking for the right reasons. My friend thinks that I have an aversion to commitment, but that can't possibly be right."

Stopping to take a deep breathe, she recognized the look on his face. She was babbling. Trying to clarify things, she started again. "Marriage is a big step, and I think both parties should really give it some serious thought. I mean, you're just supposed to do it *once*, right? My parents got divorced. Some kids might be messed up over that, but not me. I'm an adult. I realize that my parents were unhappy. The fact that they were fighting because of decisions that I made to change things is completely irrelevant. People get divorced. They get divorced all the time, but I don't want to get divorced."

Realizing that she was starting to sound like her sister, Olivia stopped. "So, what are you here for?"

The man looked confused. "I'm not sure. I thought I was going to pick out an engagement ring for my girlfriend."

Crap. "Oh, I bet you have great taste. You're wearing that excellently tailored suit, and I'm sure your girlfriend is just amazing, and you'll pick out the perfect ring, and you two will just live happily ever after. Congratulations," she finished lamely and turned her head to stare at the wall. What was wrong with her? An hour ago, she had been feeling so good, and now she was a bumbling idiot.

Thankfully, Julie returned. "All right. It looks like this was purchased almost two years ago by a J. Kennedy."

Jacob. Two years ago, Jacob was with Yvette, which meant that he'd purchased the ring for her.

Swallowing hard, she stared at the ring in her hand and willed herself not to cry. Did Jacob rip it off her finger after he'd killed her? Did he throw it in a rage? Is that what relationships came to when proposals and weddings didn't go well?

Tracing her finger lightly over the photo, Olivia took a deep breath. That wouldn't happen to her and Andrew. She'd have a talk with him, and he would understand. Just like he understood that she couldn't move in with him.

Not for the first time, she wondered how many times Andrew would understand.

Unable to look at the photo anymore, Olivia turned it over and stopped. The photo on the other side was also familiar.

"That's Samantha's ring," Olivia whispered as she stared at it. Rage burned inside her. Was there no thought put into Jacob's next engagement ring? Two years later, he simply chose the very next one in the book?

"Why yes, Samantha just fell in love with that one," Julie said brightly. "Don't you just love it? I think it's the most gorgeous diamond that we have in the store. If you're interested in one yourself, we have plenty of ways that we can personalize it, just for you."

Of course Samantha fell in love with the diamond. She would have loved anything that Jacob gave her. Would she be Jacob's next victim? Thanking Julie, Olivia slowly walked out of the store. A dark cloud had settled over her head. It looked like the case was finally solved, but not in the way that Olivia had hoped.

As she had promised, Olivia slipped the ring into her pocket and headed straight for the sheriff's station.

CHAPTER NINETEEN

Andrew pocketed Olivia's new phone and headed to his car. He was curious about what Olivia had discovered about the ring, and since he couldn't call her, he did the next best thing and called Nick. Knowing that Olivia would do as she promised, he assumed that she'd take the ring straight to the sheriff if it was important to the case.

"Andrew," Nick answered in his husky voice. He sounded even more tired, if that was possible. "I guess you're wondering if that tip panned out. One of these days, you're going to have to let me know how Olivia came by that information."

"And when you're retired, and this whole mess is behind us, I'll tell you. I actually called to see if Olivia stopped by. We found a ring outside of where Yvette's food truck used to be parked, and Celeste, of all people, hinted that the ring might have belonged to Yvette."

"You asked Celeste about the origins of a ring?" Nick asked in a perplexed voice. "Olivia must really be feeling desperate."

"No!" Andrew laughed as he navigated traffic. "It's a long story. Olivia actually took it to Stanley's to see if he could identify the buyer. She promised to take it straight to you if it belonged to Yvette, and since her phone is broken, I can't call her to ask what she discovered."

"She's not here," Nick sighed, "but I had to let Jacob go."

"Let him go? Did he lawyer up?" Andrew started to panic. If Jacob was free, he could go after Olivia again, and this time, he might succeed. "Have you lost your mind? He'll kill her!"

"It's not Jacob," Nick insisted. "He has an airtight alibi for the morning that Olivia was nearly run over. He was talking to the manager of the condo facility because he's planning on selling the place. The whole office confirmed it, and when I confronted him about the contract that I pulled from his law team and the photos on his computer, the man fell apart. He was practically in tears. Apparently, Jacob only drew up the contract in the first place to force Yvette to finally make a commitment. He said that when he realized that Yvette's free spirit had nothing to do with him, he tore up the contract, and the lawyers confirmed that as well."

Andrew frowned. "That's one hell of a move."

"You're telling me. If I ever tried something like that with Mary, I'd be out on the street. But Yvette was desperate to expand her business. Somehow, in the renegotiations of the contract, Yvette finally broke down and told him that she still loved him, but she was terrified that they weren't going to work out. According to Jacob, he'd finally decided to set Yvette free and see if she truly loved him enough to make it work. He was willing to be with her without a marriage. Andrew, you should have seen him. I've never seen a man so broken before. He said the last thing he got from

Yvette was a message saying that she didn't want to be with him anymore because she knew that he deserved better. That was sent the morning of her murder. In fact, according to the lab, it was probably sent right at the time of her death, give or take a few minutes."

"That text could have set Jacob off," Andrew insisted. "He doesn't have an alibi for the murder."

"He claimed that he was supposed to meet with Tiki, but she was sick that morning. She confirmed it. Instead, he went to his father's to get advice about expanding the food truck business. That's what Franklin told me. And if Jacob were with Yvette during the time of her murder, she wouldn't have needed to text him. She would have just told him."

Andrew gripped the steering wheel and tried to sort through the problem. "Okay, but Olivia wasn't in any danger until after she discovered that contract of Jacob's. Who else would be threatened by that?"

As soon as the words were out of his mouth, horror dawned on him. "Oh, God. Why didn't we see it before?"

"Andrew?"

"You need to find Olivia right now—before she makes a horrible mistake."

Halfway to the sheriff's office Olivia's ankle started to ache. Wishing now that she'd allowed Andrew to get her that ankle brace, she hobbled the rest of the way to Happy Endings and stopped in to rest. Chances were good that Nick already had Jacob in custody, so it wasn't like there was any huge rush to get the ring to him.

"Olivia!" her sister gasped. "I've been trying to call you all day! Jackie told me what happened."

"Did she also tell you that my phone was broken?"

Janelle pulled up short and frowned. "Yes. Now that I think about it, she did. What did Nick say? Does he think that it's connected to the case?"

"Does he think that my amateur sleuthing nearly got me run over? Yes, he might have mentioned that," Olivia said dryly.

Janelle's eyes widened in fear. "Oh, God. Did you tell him that we broke into Jacob's condo? Olivia, I can't go to jail. I'm not strong enough. I wouldn't make it, and I do not look good in orange."

"Janelle, you're not going to jail," Olivia sighed, sinking into the nearest chair. "Andrew passed along the information without telling him what we did, so you can relax. Do you think I could get some ice for my ankle? It's killing me."

"Right away!" Janelle said, and hurried into the back, returning quickly. "You poor thing," she sympathized, brandishing a scone in one hand and a towel-wrapped bag of ice in the other. "I bet you're in so much pain. This should be a lesson to you. Don't stick your nose where it doesn't belong."

"You're not wrong." As Janelle adjusted the ice bag on Olivia's ankle, Olivia took a bite of the scone and moaned in pleasure. "But you'd be lying if you didn't admit that you had some fun the other night."

"I was mortified when I woke up the next morning, and I had a terrible hangover, but Patrick just laughed it off. I still haven't told him, and I feel terrible about it. We don't keep secrets from each other."

Olivia shrugged. "I'm sure there's no harm in telling him now. He might even see you in a whole new light. It might freshen up your marriage a bit!"

"My marriage does not need freshening," Janelle said frostily. "And I take offense to you suggesting that."

"Please. You may have date night once a week, but you always go to the same place. When was the last time you took a vacation? Even Mom is taking romantic vacations," Olivia pointed out.

Janelle grimaced. "You might be right, but with the money that I'm putting into the business, we don't exactly have anything left over for a vacation. Still, it probably wouldn't hurt to switch things up a bit. Where are you going, anyway? You don't have any dogs with you. Did you finally lose them all?"

"Are you suggesting that I'm a bad dog walker?"

"I'm suggesting that a woman who can't even keep her own dog contained has no business walking anyone else's," Janelle pointed out.

"No dog-walking business, no need for an office upstairs," Olivia teased. "No, we found this ring this morning by Yvette's. Stanley's daughter just identified it as Yvette's, so I'm taking it to Nick. It's awful. Jacob must have either demanded the ring back or taken it back after he killed her. Maybe that was what set him off to begin with. I'm sure it wasn't easy seeing her with the ring after what she did to him."

Janelle shuddered. "I just never could imagine Jacob with a temper. Even after the whole wedding scandal, Jacob never had a bad word to say about Yvette."

"Get this. So I found Yvette's ring in the display book at Stanley's, and the very next ring showcased? It's the ring that Samantha was flashing around the other day. Stanley's daughter said that Samantha loved it. I've never thought that I would feel

221

bad for Samantha, but she has no idea what kind of man she's promised to marry." Olivia repositioned the ice on her ankle and winced.

Janelle frowned. "You shouldn't be alone until this whole thing is over. Where's Andrew?"

Olivia gingerly massaged her ankle. "He went to get me a new phone. He's so sweet, and we don't have anything to worry about. Nick was going to pick up Jacob this morning after Andrew spoke to him. There's no way that Jacob is out walking free, but it's nice that you're worrying about me."

"Of course I worry about you, Olivia. You're my baby sister, and I love you." Janelle hugged her. "I know that things haven't been easy between us, but I think that things are going to be different now. And despite all the changes that you're facing, you need to remember that Andrew loves you. You should appreciate that more," Janelle warned.

Olivia just stared at her. It had been a long time since she heard Janelle try to give her some sisterly advice rather than just steamroll over her with opinions.

Janelle continued to cluck at her. Her older sister didn't seem to understand the significance of this moment between them.

Then Olivia looked out the window and gasped. "Oh dear. Here comes Samantha. I wonder how she's dealing with all of this? To think that after all this time, she and Jacob are finally engaged, and he's a murderer!"

The bell rang as the door swung open, and Samantha popped in. She was dressed in a gorgeous dark gray skirt with a baby blue blouse. She was wearing the diamond ring on a fine chain around her neck and immediately pulled it out and fiddled with it as she walked in the store. The gem caught the sunlight and sparkled. It was hard to miss. "Hello, ladies!"

Janelle shook her head. "Samantha, darling. I am so sorry."

If Olivia could have reached, she would have kicked her older sister. It wasn't their business to tell Samantha the truth about her fiancée. Samantha looked at them in puzzlement. "Why are you sorry?"

"Janelle is out of those muffins that you like so much," Olivia said hurriedly. She gave her sister a pointed look. The last thing she wanted to deal with today was a hysterical Samantha.

The woman bought the excuse and frowned. "Oh, Jacob will be so disappointed. He said he had something big to tell me, so I thought I'd get him one of those muffins that he likes so much. I certainly don't eat them. Too many carbs."

Janelle looked offended, but Olivia opened her mouth before her sister could speak. "He has something big to tell you?"

"Yes, although I can't imagine what that could be. After all, he's already popped the question. That's supposed to be a secret, but I'm sure you two won't spill the beans. I'll be so happy when I can finally wear the ring on my finger rather than hanging it around my neck. He called me a few minutes ago. He's going to meet me here."

Worried, Olivia stared at her. "Wait, he called you a few minutes ago? Where was he?"

"He didn't say. Does it matter? You're not about to close, are you?"

"Samantha, sweetheart," Janelle said softly. "Maybe you should sit down." She exchanged a worried look with Olivia, and Olivia knew exactly what her sister was thinking. Samantha had no idea what Jacob had done. She was about to be crushed.

But Olivia wasn't thinking about Samantha's feelings. She was listening to the voice of alarm inside her head. Something wasn't fitting together. It shouldn't have been possible for Jacob to call her. Jacob should have been in custody. What was going on?

"Why? It's okay if you don't have the muffins. Some chocolate chip cookies will be just as nice," Samantha said as she pulled out a chair.

Slowly, Olivia pushed the emerald ring toward the sunlight so that the sun would catch it. Her mind raced. The only reason that

Nick would let Jacob go was if he were innocent. A solid alibi? And if Jacob hadn't murdered Yvette in vengeance, there was only one other explanation.

Samantha's eyes swept over Olivia's table, and her whole body went rigid.

Olivia saw the woman's demeanor change, and the answer to the mystery finally slammed into place. Gone was the happily engaged woman. In its place sat a cold-blooded killer.

"Janelle, why don't you go check on the goods that you have in the oven," Olivia said quietly.

"I don't have anything in the oven," Janelle said with a puzzled look.

"Janelle's not going anywhere, and neither are you," Samantha said icily, her eyes fixed on the ring. She reached into her purse and slowly pulled out a gun. "I guess I didn't throw it far enough."

"You were the one who tried to run me over," Olivia whispered. "How did you know that we were in the condo?"

Samantha's eyes were terrifyingly cold as she dropped all pretense of pleasantries. As she pointed the weapon at Olivia, there was no hesitation, nor remorse, in her face. "There was a dusting of flour in the kitchen. Jacob doesn't bake, and your sister is always covered in the stuff. Plus, the tablet has a safety feature that takes a picture of whoever wakes it up from sleep mode. I'm just lucky that I used it before Jacob."

"Samantha?" Janelle gasped. "What are you doing? Why are you carrying a gun?"

Samantha kept her eyes trained on Olivia. "When I didn't get the job done the first time around, I knew that I needed to be ready. I don't know what you found in that condo to link to me, but I knew if you were there, you were getting close," she said nastily.

"But we weren't there for you," Olivia said, slowly standing to her feet. The bag of ice fell to the floor. Her ankle throbbed, but if she was to face a deranged killer, she wasn't going to do it sitting down. "We thought it was Jacob. I already turned the evidence over to Nick. Jacob's in custody for Yvette's murder."

The pain on Samantha's face was evident, and Olivia knew that no matter what Samantha did—or had done—her love for Jacob was true. "No." The gun stayed steady as the woman shook her head. "Nick won't arrest Jacob. Everyone knows that Jacob is a good man. It'll be fine. Nick will let Jacob go, and we'll finally be together. We'll finally get married like we're supposed to."

Olivia took a deep breath. Her eyes darted to the movement behind Samantha, but the woman just stared straight at her. She needed to get a full confession out of Samantha. "You wanted everyone to think that you and Jacob were back together after

Yvette left him, but that wasn't true, was it? He turned to you because you were friends, but it wasn't anything more than that. And when you found out that Jacob and Yvette were back together, you lost control."

"They were not back together!" Samantha screamed. "You're lying! Jacob wouldn't do that to me. Not again—but I knew what was happening. I knew that she was using her business to lure Jacob back. She was trying to steal him away from me again, trying to destroy him. Jacob and I are the heart of this town, we're the Lexingburg Sweethearts, and I was not going to let her ruin that again."

"But they were together," Olivia said carefully as she tried to put herself between Samantha and Janelle. She would never forgive herself if she got her sister hurt because she couldn't leave well enough alone. "There were pictures to prove that Jacob was with Yvette just a few weeks ago. They were in love, and Yvette just didn't know how to take that last step."

"It doesn't matter," Samantha hissed. "She's dead, and I sent him a text from her phone that morning. He knows they're over. Now we're together. I have his ring. I have it—and not her!"

"But that's not his ring, is it?" Olivia asked quietly, her eyes steady on the other woman's face. She needed to ground Samantha to reality and pull her out of this fantasy. "You bought that ring yourself. That's why you don't want anyone to see it. Jacob hasn't

227

proposed to you yet."

"Shut up!" Samantha screamed. "He doesn't have to tell me that he loves me. He doesn't have to ask me to marry him. I know what's in his heart! I know what he wants."

"The dinner at L'Amore," Olivia continued. "The big night on the town. You're playing on Jacob's vulnerability in order to win him back. You want to be the shoulder that he cries on."

"I was there when she walked away from him," Samantha spat. "I would never leave him. She would only have broken his heart again, but not me. I'll be there forever, and he'll see that. We're going to be happy together, now that Yvette isn't in the picture anymore. I did what I had to do."

She was so lost in her own rage that she hadn't heard the door open. Jacob stood behind her, a look of horror on his face. "Samantha, what did you do?"

"She has a gun!" Olivia cried out in warning.

Samantha whirled around. "Jacob!" she gasped in surprise. "Baby. Don't listen to them. They're just spreading lies. They're trying to break us up because they're jealous. They're jealous of my happy ending."

"What happy ending? What are you talking about?"

Samantha pointed to her ring. "Our happy ending. See? We're

going to be so happy, baby. Isn't that why you asked me here today? You were going to tell me that you love me, right?"

"No, I wasn't. I was going to tell you that I took your advice and sold the condo. I'm buying a house," Jacob said tonelessly, as if in shock. "A fresh start, just like you suggested." He paused. "You killed Yvette?" he asked her, his voice suddenly hoarse. "I don't understand. We weren't even together."

"You bought a house?" Samantha asked wildly. "That's great, honey. I love that house. We're going to be so happy living there. You realize that, right? Yvette was a mistake. We should have gotten married as soon as we turned eighteen, but you wanted to wait until after we went to college. So I waited, and then you came back and said that you weren't sure about us. So I gave you space, and you ran to her! She was a nobody. A drifter, and you gave her my ring!"

"Samantha," Jacob said calmly, but the woman kept going.

"You gave her my wedding, and when she didn't show up, you still couldn't get over her! I have been here for you. I've always been here for you, baby. I saw what she was doing to you. I just went to talk to her. I just wanted to convince her to leave town, but she said these horrible things, and I just had to protect you. I had to protect *us*. This is our chance to correct that mistake. That's what you want, right?"

Jacob shook his head. "There is no *us*, Samantha. I had no idea what our friendship was doing to you. I'm sorry—I'm so sorry."

"No!" Samantha screamed in rage and raised the gun again. This time, Olivia was ready. She threw herself at the woman; they both hit the ground, hard, and the gun flew across the floor. Pain lanced up her leg, and Olivia groaned as Samantha scrambled away from her.

Samantha, no longer concerned with Olivia or Janelle, launched herself at Jacob with a banshee scream, but he caught her easily as she crumpled. She was still on the floor, sobbing, when Nick pulled up.

"Jacob!" he gasped when he burst through the door. "Let her go."

When Jacob released Samantha, she crumpled to the floor in tears, a sobbing heap of misery.

Janelle reached down and gingerly picked up the gun. "She's insane," she murmured as she handed the weapon to Nick.

"Are you okay?" he asked Olivia as he handcuffed Samantha. Janelle reached down and helped her sister up.

"Yeah," Olivia said slowly, leaning on Janelle as she stared at the mascara trekking down Samantha's tear-streaked face. "I was on my way to give you this ring that I found. What are you doing here? How did you know it was Samantha?"

"I didn't," the sheriff admitted. "Andrew put it together. He called me to see if you'd gotten the ring to me. When we realized that Jacob wasn't the killer, he put two and two together. Your boyfriend has a knack for this kind of thing."

"Of course he does," Olivia muttered, but she smiled. She was proud of Andrew.

Samantha looked as if she was in a trance as Nick pulled her to her feet. "I did it for you, baby," she whispered, over and over again.

Jacob didn't say anything as he followed Nick out of the bakery, but Olivia could see the pain in his face. In less than a week, Jacob had lost the woman that he loved—and his best friend. It would take a long time before he healed.

"After all this, and Andrew solved the case before I did," Olivia muttered. "I am seriously the worst detective ever."

Janelle patted her on the shoulder sympathetically. "That's what we've all been trying to tell you."

CHAPTER TWENTY

Olivia figured the news of Samantha's arrest would destroy Lexingburg, but Andrew predicted that the town would bounce back in no time.

As usual, he was right.

For the first couple of days, the murder was all anyone could talk about. Franklin Kennedy returned from Florida. Apparently, he'd tried to convince Jacob to move with them, but Jacob wasn't running, although no one had seen much of him. Olivia knew that he was trying to assemble a team of lawyers and doctors to help Samantha. She was clearly mentally imbalanced, and guilt rested heavily on Jacob's shoulders. Although everyone tried to tell him that it wasn't his fault, he privately told Nick and Olivia that he'd always known something was off with Samantha. It was the reason he'd broken up with her in the first place. He insisted that he should have gotten her some help to begin with, and maybe none of this would have happened.

In light of everything, he wasn't entirely sure if he was going to go through with the Jump Start coffee truck expansion or not. He told Olivia that he had some soul-searching to do.

Although he'd complained about her meddling, Franklin agreed that Olivia's actions had saved his son, As a thank-you, he agreed to make the necessary repairs to the brownstone before starting the sales process. It would give them more time and meant that Janelle would stop pressuring her, and they could finally do some research and see if it really was the best move. Olivia explained the risk of such an impulsive buy, and Janelle grudgingly agreed to wait and see how Franklin handled the repairs.

Celeste was having an excellent time with her pet psychic sideline. Olivia found her missing socks under Goodwin's bed, and even though Andrew tried to remind her that there weren't many other places they could have been, she privately wondered if Celeste might have found her true calling. Not only were Olivia's previous clients asking for Olivia to take their pets to Celeste, the news managed to increase Olivia's business, also. She had so many people calling her that she even began to wonder if she should hire an employee or two to help her out.

When Fender didn't immediately prove to be the declaration of love that Douglas had hoped he would be, he shoved the poor dog at Olivia. Andrew balked at adding another dog to the mix, but Olivia didn't have the heart to take the poor old thing to the adoption agency. She promised Andrew that if she found a good home for him, she'd give him up, but privately, she was certain that Fender wouldn't live longer than a week. How the old dog had managed to make it this long was beyond her.

She finished her audiobook (Rose's grandmother's loving gardener was the mastermind) and decided to give the Rose Palmer mysteries a rest. Maybe she'd try one of Jackie's romance books and see what all the fuss was about.

It was a full week after the arrest before everything started to feel more normal. Nick was still lying to his wife about Tucker, but he was looking much better now that the case was closed. Snowball was still happy in his tiaras and tutus, and Lily still wanted to dig into everything. The canine crew didn't mind having Fender along, and the more the old dog walked, the faster he became. He even started to pick up some bad habits from Goodwin. Soon Olivia would have two thieves to contend with.

That Saturday, with no dogs to walk, Olivia leashed Goodwin and Fender and headed out to the dog park with Andrew. Once inside the gate, she unleashed the dogs so they could run free while she and Andrew strolled along the perimeter toward the white gazebo in the middle of the park.

"I sort of envied Yvette," Olivia admitted quietly.

"God, why?"

"She always seemed to have it so easy. Even when the scandal with Jacob broke out, she didn't seem to care. She had her business, and that always seemed to be enough for her. Do you think she really loved him?"

"I do," Andrew said quietly. "You didn't see the photos. She looked genuinely happy just to be with him. I think they probably could have made it work."

"She abandoned him at the altar. How do you get over that?" She shook her head in amazement.

"Sometimes, you just have to adapt to be with the woman that you love," Andrew explained. "Jacob wanted to spend the rest of his life with Yvette, and he realized that he had been going about it the wrong way. He didn't have to marry her to have her, and he was willing to be happy with that."

Olivia looked up and studied his face. "You feel that way about me, don't you?" she asked, with dismay in her voice. "You have to adapt to be with me."

"You say that like it's a bad thing," he said with a smile as he tucked a flyaway hair behind her ear. "Every relationship has its give-and-take. I do have to make some changes to be with you, but the reward is always worth it."

"You don't want to change me? You asked me time and time again to stay away from the investigation."

"I knew when I told you to stay away from Yvette's case that you probably weren't going to, and I did see the effort that you made to try."

"But you weren't even mad when I broke my promise," she said sullenly. "You're never mad."

"Actually, I was furious," he admitted. "But more than furious, I was terrified. You can get so wrapped up in something that you don't even see the world around you, and I didn't want you to get hurt. But getting mad at you wasn't going to solve anything. I don't want to be the man who keeps you from doing what you want, Olivia. Even if I don't think it's a good idea. You did get hurt, but you also caught a killer who might have otherwise gotten away. All that I can hope to be is the man who helps you when things don't go the way you planned."

It was probably the sweetest, most romantic, and most honest thing he'd ever said. Olivia turned to gaze at the gazebo while she tried to think of a response, but for the first time ever, her mind was completely blank. It was so obvious that Andrew was the perfect man for her, but she couldn't help but wonder if she was the perfect woman for him.

"Andrew, do you think of me as an investment?"

"Excuse me?" he asked warily.

"Like, do you put up with me because you've already put so much time and energy into me?"

When he laughed in response, her eyes narrowed. Did he understand that her concern was serous?

He shook his head, then sobered. "Olivia, is this what's been bothering you? What on earth would make you think that?"

"I know you're blind to it, but half the female population in this town wants you, and I know what a pain I am. Sometimes I don't understand why you put up with me."

"Sweetheart, I don't put up with you at all. I love you, and I accept you exactly as you are. I stay with you because you make me happy. If this wasn't working, I'd walk away. Don't ever doubt that."

It was exactly what she wanted to hear, and every muscle in her body relaxed. For the first time in a long time, she actually felt content.

They reached the gazebo, and she relaxed against one of the white columns and smiled as she watched the other dogs play.

Something cold and wet pushed into her hand, and she absently scratched at Goodwin's muzzle. He whined and pushed his whole body against her. Puzzled, Olivia looked down. "What's wrong, buddy?"

He wouldn't stop moving, and she reached down to grab his collar and keep him still so she could figure out if he was injured. This was his time to romp and play, and it wasn't like him to stay glued to her side. Kneeling down, she ran her fingers over his fur. "Andrew, I think something is wrong."

"Nothing is wrong, baby," he said softly.

237

Puzzled, she raised her gaze and stared at him. There was something unusual in his expression. She was about the demand that he help her when her hands ran under Goodwin's neck. As she touched the strange object, her whole body went still.

There was nothing wrong with Goodwin.

Holding her breath, she turned the collar until the glint of the diamond hit the light.

Oval cut with a platinum setting. Simple. Beautiful. Perfect.

Laughing hoarsely, she stood. "I can't even get Goodwin to learn to stay, but you somehow trained him to do this. How did you do it? Hand signal?"

"A man never reveals his secrets," he said from behind her.

A thrill ran through her, and she closed her eyes. "Andrew."

"I found that ring when I was in high school," Andrew said quietly.

Olivia turned her head and saw that he was on one knee.

"I didn't tell anyone because I knew that ring would lead me to the woman that I wanted to spend the rest of my life with. When I took the job at Lowell Hospital, I had given up. The woman that I thought I'd loved was gone, and I was in a new state where I didn't know anyone. I couldn't stand the thought of starting over again.

The day that I met you, I had the ring in my pocket. I was going to sell it to Stanley, but Goodwin intervened. Being with you made my life complete, and I know that *you* know I've been trying to propose. I know that you're panicked about the thought, and I know that you've been dodging this moment—but I am not Jacob, and you are not Yvette."

The world drifted away as she stared at him. Since the moment she'd suspected that he was about to propose, she'd imagined this moment. She'd had no idea how she'd feel, and even now, as he spoke, emotions warred inside her. Relief that the moment had finally come. Anticipation for what he would say next. Terror over how she would respond.

"I know that I'm going to spend the rest of my life with you, and I know that I don't need a marriage to do that, but I also know you. You're terrified of commitment, but if you don't take the dive, you're always going to wonder about our future. You'll second-guess why I didn't ask you. You'll wonder if we're meant to be together if we're not married. So, Olivia Rickard, I'm telling you that I love you, here and forever. I am promising you that no matter what, I will always be here for you, and I accept you exactly as you are. And I'm going to ask you that question that you've been dreading for weeks now, and hopefully, once I ask it, you'll realize that you have nothing to fear."

Oh, God. This is it.

"Will you marry me?"

END OF

"BARKING UP THE WRONG BAKERY"

HAPPY TAILS DOG WALKING MYSTERIES

BOOK ONE

PS: Book Two of Stella St. Claire's, Happy Tails Dog Walking Mysteries, is out now. Get your copy of **Till Death do us Bark** at www.StellaStClaire.com.

CONNECT WITH STELLA!

Stella lives and breathes cozy mysteries! With her head always buried inside these books, it's no wonder that she would put pen to paper to bring her own cozy mysteries to life. The words flew onto the page, and she's already teeming with ideas for the next series.

With her trusted canine by her side, it seemed only natural to be inspired by her beautiful beagle Doogle and the many hours they spent walking through scenic New England villages. When Stella's not reading books, she's off on road trips, exploring every nook and cranny in neighboring towns, seeking inspiration for her next book.

She's keen to see what her fellow cozy critics think of "Happy Tails Dog Walker Mysteries," so leave a review and share your thoughts!

Please leave feedback for Stella on her:

Facebook: www.facebook.com/stellastclaire/

Or Goodreads:
www.goodreads.com/Stella_StClaire

MEET DOOGLE!

I would like to thank you for purchasing this book. If you would like to hear more about what I am up to, or continue to hear about Olivia's superb sleuthing—then please sign up for my mailing list at www.StellaStClaire.com.

Most importantly, you will get the cutest Beagle around hitting your inbox every month. Doogle the Beagle is my awesome canine companion and not a line of cozy mystery goodness would get written without him. He's quite a talker, so I'll let him introduce himself...

I'm no Sherlock Bones, but when it comes to Cozies, I know my stuff. Every plot pawblem Stella has, she comes to me. She talks, i listen and before you can say *Labracadabrador* she's off typing again. Stella and I are a pretty good team—even if i have to do all the hard work...

Super-healthy Pumpkin Pebbles

This treat won't just get your dog's tail wagging, it's also very good for them—filled with fiber, vitamin A, beta-carotene, potassium, and iron.

Ingredients:

- 1/2 cup canned pumpkin

- 4 tablespoon molasses (dog-safe sweetener)

- 4 tablespoon water

- 2 tablespoon vegetable oil

- 2 cups whole wheat flour

- ¼ teaspoon baking soda

- ¼ teaspoon baking powder

Instructions:

1. Preheat the oven to 350 degrees F. Line cookie sheet with parchment paper, foil or a silicon mat.

2. In a large bowl, mix the pumpkin, molasses, vegetable oil, and water together.

3. Add the whole wheat flour, baking soda, and baking powder to the mixture and stir until dough softens

4.   Scoop out small spoonfuls of dough and roll into balls on your hands (wet hands work best)

5.   Set the balls onto a lightly greased cookie sheet and flatten with a fork

6.   Bake approximately 25 minutes until dough is hardened. Check treats after 15 minutes and 20 minutes to make sure they don't get over cooked. Cooking time will depend on size and thickness of your dog treat.

7.   Store your homemade Pumpkin Pebbles in an airtight container and place them in the refrigerator or freezer. If frozen, allow the treat to thaw for 10 to 20 minutes prior to serving to your dog. Treats can last for up to 2 months in the refrigerator and 6 months in the freezer.

Stella St. Claire

EXCLUSIVE EXTRACT

The rain came down in sheets, splattering on the sidewalk and effectively clearing Main Street. A chill wrapped around Olivia Rickard as she huddled under the awning of her sister's bakery. She stamped her feet, in search of elusive warmth. In her arms, a small, displeased pug wriggled and cried. Holding him closer, she tried to tuck him into the front of her light jacket in an attempt quiet him and warm him up. The poor old dog suffered from arthritis and hated being out in the cold, but his owner demanded that the dog be walked no matter the weather. As it was, Olivia ended up carrying him most of the time, which seemed equally bothersome to Clyde. There was simply no pleasing him.

His nails scraped against her neck. "Ouch," she muttered, pushing his foot away. "Would you stop?"

Clyde grunted in answer, and Olivia promptly set him down on the wet pavement, just managing to avoid a puddle. The pug heaved a huge sigh and looked up at her through bulging eyes as though she'd betrayed him in some horrible way.

"This is not my fault," she insisted. "I'm just doing my job."

A movement caught Clyde's attention, and he barked in sharp yaps as another figure came rushing toward them. "Really, Olivia! People are going to think that you've lost your mind if you start talking to the dogs in *public*," Janelle said, juggling with her umbrella in her hurry to get her keys out. Dressed in jeans and a chef's coat, Olivia's older sister still managed to look gorgeous despite the horrible weather. Her makeup was artfully applied, highlighting her high cheekbones and smooth olive skin. A shimmery eyeliner brought out the gold flecks in her eyes, and soft pink glossed over her lips.

Olivia felt a stab of jealousy—although it was her own fault. The two sisters looked remarkably similar; not identical, of course, as Olivia was taller and Janelle curvier. The older sister wore her thick, lush hair in a cute, flippy short style. Olivia kept her hair longer so she could easily pull it back in a ponytail. Although Olivia obsessively watched makeup tutorials on YouTube, she rarely bothered with the stuff, which was part of the reason why Janelle looked spectacular, and Olivia looked like a drowned rat.

"You'd be yelling at the dog too if you had to deal with him. He's like a grumpy old man," Olivia insisted.

Shaking out her umbrella, Janelle shouldered her large tote and unlocked the bakery. Clyde immediately scampered in, and Janelle gasped. "You can't let him wander loose in there! He smells awful!"

"You're the one who wanted me to help you buy the brownstone so I could have an office above you," Olivia pointed out. "I do walk dogs for a living."

"Well, they're not allowed to run around down here. Take him upstairs while I make us some coffee," Janelle ordered, surveying the darkened room with a frown. "Where is he, anyway?"

"Clyde!" Olivia called, although she suspected that the old dog was following his nose. She had recently acquired an older dog of her own, a basset hound named Fender. Mayor Hutchinson had adopted him a couple of months ago, hoping to win the affections of Lady Celeste, the town's psychic, and when that didn't work, he had thrust the dog into Olivia's care. The poor thing was so old that Olivia had suspected he wouldn't make it more than a week, but it had turned out that Fender was much livelier than anyone might expect. While he feigned deafness and occasional blindness, he had no problems sniffing out food. He didn't even seem to mind staying at home, warm and dry and sleeping, while Olivia walked other people's dogs.

Olivia suspected that Clyde was rooting around in the storage room, and as it turned out, she was right.

"I don't understand why I had to meet you so early," she grumbled after snagging the grunting roly-poly pup. She carried him to the stairwell. "The sun is barely up."

"Maybe now that you know how early I have to get up to start baking, you'll appreciate all the treats that you steal," Janelle pointed out.

Olivia started up the stairs, feeling for the first few shadowy

249

steps until light flashed behind her, lighting the stairwell wall as her sister flipped the downstairs light switch. Even better, she heard the splashing sound of her sister pouring water into the well of the bakery's coffee machine. Her sister's voice called up to her, "Besides, you're so busy with wedding planning, it's hard to get you to stand still long enough to actually *talk* to you."

Content to be inside and warm, Clyde curled up in one of the many dog's beds strewn about upstairs.

Listening to Janelle's ranting, faint as it was, drifting up through the stairwell, Olivia couldn't help but glance down at the ring on her finger. For weeks, she'd dodged Andrew's proposal because she'd been unsure if she was ready, but once the question was out, there was only one answer.

Yes.

"I would think that you'd be happy," Olivia called, slamming the door to keep the dog in. She jogged down the stairs. Reaching the bottom, she lowered her voice to a conversational tone. "After all, you were the one who went behind my back to team up with Andrew in his scheme to propose."

Janelle shot her a disapproving look. "Really, Olivia, you're being ridiculous. It's a proposal, not an act of treason. I just tried to help things along. You're happy now, so what's the big deal?"

Olivia knew how difficult it was for Janelle to admit that she was wrong, but her big sister had wanted a romantic proposal for Olivia, and even though things hadn't gone to her plan, the proposal had ended up being just perfect for Olivia. Strangely enough, now that Olivia was in planning mode, her sister never seemed to want to talk about the wedding. Frustrating. "I'm here now, so why don't you just tell me what you need."

The smell of coffee filled the small bakery, and Olivia watched it brew with fierce concentration. She would agree to just about anything to get a cup. Her sister's text to meet her this morning had been unwelcome, but she'd already been up—Since the wedding preparations had begun, Olivia hadn't gotten much sleep.

"Sign these. Right now," Janelle said suddenly. Her voice had a sharp impatient edge that shook Olivia out of her stupor.

Blinking, she turned her head and stared at her sister. "What?"

"You've dragged your feet every step of the way during the buying process, Olivia, but the time for procrastinating is over. Now, Franklin has patched the roof and fixed the pipes. You have no other reason to stall, so we have to sign so we can start the closing process. Otherwise, in a week, Franklin can go with another bid."

"It's not stalling," Olivia argued. "It's making a good decision when it comes to a huge purchase." She eyed her sister narrowly. "Sometimes I think there isn't a hesitant bone in your body. You

251

decide that you want something, and you go right for it without considering all the options." There had been a time she'd doubted her decision to buy the brownstone with Janelle. Her sister had rented this piece of prime real estate for a year to get her bakery up and running, and when the landlord had offered to sell it to her, she'd jumped at the chance. Unfortunately, Janelle didn't have the money to buy it herself and assumed that Olivia would help.

Buying the brownstone would make it harder for Olivia to leave the small town that she had grown up in. Even worse, the thought of going into business with her sister had horrified her—but things had changed.

Together, Olivia and Janelle faced the crazed killer of Yvette Dunn and managed to bond.

Olivia had found the strength to tell her sister the truth, and Janelle had agreed to be more cautious about the sale.

In fact, her sister had taken all of her advice. But now . . .

"I'm not signing anything without reading it," Olivia said, reaching for the papers. "But I'll look them over before the deadline. I see that you've signed them. Did you bother to read them?"

"It's a standard contract of sale, Olivia. Don't be so paranoid!" Grabbing some paper cups from the cabinet, Janelle slid one into a cardboard sleeve and poured out steaming coffee. "Promise me that you'll look them over tonight."

"I don't know if I'll get a chance to do it tonight. I have another meeting with Lacy to discuss flowers. I thought I wanted lilies, but now I'm not so sure." It turned out that planning a wedding was a complicated affair. Olivia had all been ready to just marry Andrew in the courthouse, but everyone else in the world had dug their heels in at her suggestion. So she'd started tentatively planning a wedding, only to discover that it was a horrendous affair. She'd hired the best, Lacy McBride, to help her get everything put together. Olivia had never been much of a girlie-girl, but she suddenly had the urge to plan the perfect wedding.

Maybe it was just the competitive side of her talking.

Inhaling the comforting aroma of the coffee, Olivia closed her eyes and took the first sip. As the warm liquid slid down her throat, she felt instantly more amiable.

"I think you have a problem," Janelle muttered. "You are addicted to caffeine."

Olivia just shrugged and smiled. "You didn't make the whole pot just for me. I'll see if I can't look at the papers before the end of the week. You could have given them to me this afternoon."

"Like I said, you've been busy."

"You could have given them to Mom. She seems to have no

problems hunting me down." Pamela Rickard had been overjoyed that her youngest daughter was finally getting married, and she'd thrown herself into the wedding planning. She hadn't minced words in expressing her displeasure when Olivia had hired a wedding planner, and Olivia's mother and Lacy had done nothing but butt heads since the very beginning.

The rain had eased up, and Olivia headed back up the steps to retrieve Clyde. "I've got a few other dogs that I need to walk this morning. I'll call you as soon as I look over the papers."

"Sign them and you'll have a dry place to keep the dogs rather than forcing them run in the rain," Janelle reminded her smugly.

"Yeah, yeah." Clyde moaned in despair as Olivia carried him down the stairs. She tucked him easily under his arm and ignored his protests. "See you later, sis!"

Outside, she glanced at the sky in speculation. Although it was only drizzling, the clouds looked as though they were merely taking a break. It was a good ten-minute jog to Clyde's owners house, and Olivia wasn't really one to jog.

"Olivia!"

Whipping her head around, she saw Andrew walk briskly toward her. Smiling, she took a moment to drink him in.

Andrew Patterson was one of the handsomest men she'd ever met. A newcomer in Happy Corner, he'd moved from

Connecticut to head the IT department at the hospital in Lowell, a neighboring city. He was a few years older than Olivia. His shaggy dark hair was perfect for running her fingers through, his dark smoldering eyes sometimes took her breath away, and his impish smile melted her heart. Although she had been hesitant at every step in their relationship, he never seemed to doubt her for an instant.

"My, isn't this a surprise?" she said flirtatiously as she put Clyde down and embraced Andrew. "You can't go more than few hours without me?"

Rather than playing along, he just frowned and drew something out of his coat pocket. "Olivia, what is this?"

Confused, she glanced down at the brochure in his hand.

He was upset. That was rare.

"That's the brochure for the wedding venue. Isn't it gorgeous?"

"Gorgeous? Olivia, it's four hours away. Why do we need to travel so far to get married?"

All the doubts Lacy had been able to dismiss with a wave of her beautifully manicured hand came rushing back. Olivia blinked and marshalled Lacy's arguments. "Lacy just purchased some shares on the land. That gives her clients first choice when picking a date. I know it's a bit of a drive, but people travel all over the country to get married there. It's got a gorgeous view of the river, several ballrooms for entertaining, and rooms for the guests to stay in, not to mention that we're getting a great deal. I thought that you'd love it?" In an attempt to soothe him, she reached up and pressed her hand to his chest.

Normally, when she did that, he'd take her hand and kiss her fingers, but this time, he just shook his head.

"Why are you moving so fast to plan this wedding? I told you that I'd give you all the time you wanted during the engagement. I know how you are about change."

He wasn't wrong. Normally, Olivia hated change, and for a while, the thought of getting married had made her break out in hives. It didn't help that the whole town was watching her and making bets on whether she'd go through with it. Until Andrew had come along, Olivia had been notorious for breaking up with her boyfriends before their one-year anniversary, but the wedding-planning process—especially since she'd hired Lacy— had gone smoothly.

Lacy had pointed out the obvious. The sooner they had the wedding, the sooner it would be over.

"This is just how Lacy gets things done. I don't have any doubts about marrying you, Andrew. I just want to do it as soon as possible. Don't you feel the same?"

He ignored her question. "We need to sit down and talk

tonight, Olivia. We had a budget set up for a longer engagement. We can't afford to get married this quickly."

Puzzled, she cocked her head. Was he suggesting that they couldn't afford the wedding she'd spent so much time meticulously planning?

Silence fell between them, and he finally sighed. "Why don't I give you and Clyde a ride back? The weather doesn't look like it's going to hold much longer."

"Don't you have to go to work?"

"I have time, Olivia. We have time."

The implication was clear, but she didn't acknowledge it. Instead, she bent and gathered Clyde back into her arms, and they headed to Andrew's car. The drive back was silent as Olivia tried to collect her thoughts. Everyone was pushing her to get married, and now that she'd embraced the traditions of wedding planning, she couldn't seem to make anyone happy. Her own mother wasn't speaking to her, her sister didn't seem to care, and now even Andrew was upset with her.

Andrew was never upset. Even when she'd investigated Yvette's murder—after he'd told her not to—he didn't get angry. When Samantha had nearly run her over, he still hadn't yelled at her. But now, when she was throwing herself headfirst into wedding planning, he wanted to argue about things?

How backwards was that?

And it didn't escape her notice that when she'd asked if he wanted to marry her, he'd ignored the question.

She knew that Andrew loved her.

It wasn't possible that he was getting cold feet—was it?

Get your copy of **Till Death do us Bark** at www.StellaStClaire.com.

Made in the USA
Columbia, SC
14 January 2018